• •

AIR RAID

T0160051

THE
SEAGULL
LIBRARY OF
GERMAN
LITERATURE

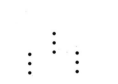

ALEXANDER KLUGE

The Air Raid on Halberstadt on 8 April 1945

TRANSLATED BY MARTIN CHALMERS

LONDON NEW YORK CALCUTTA

This publication was supported by a grant from
the Goethe-Institut, India

• • •

Seagull Books, 2022

ISBN 978 1 8030 9 036 8

British Library Cataloguing-in-Publication Data
A catalogue record for this book is available from the British Library

Typeset by Seagull Books, Calcutta, India
Printed and bound by WordsWorth India, New Delhi, India

CONTENTS

The Air Raid on Halberstadt on 8 April 1945   1

What Does 'Really' Mean in Retrospect?
17 More Stories About the Air War

Dragonflies of Death   87

Commentary on 'Dragonflies of Death'   90

The Dragonfly   91

The Long Paths to Knowledge   92

What Does 'Really' Mean in Retrospect?   93

Love 1944   94

Cooperative Behaviour   95

Fires inside People   96

Zoo Animals in the Air Raids   97

What Holds Voluntary Actions Together?   99

Fire-Brigade Commander W. Schönecke Reports   106

The Run-Up to the Catastrophe   110

Inexplicable Reactions in Sandstone Rock   115

How the 'Flying Fortresses' Disappeared in Lake Constance   117

The Gleam in the Enemy's Eye   119

Total Toothache   120

News of Star Wars   123

Between History and Natural History.
On the Literary Description of Total Destruction.
Remarks on Kluge   125
W. G. SEBALD

Sources   137

. . .
. . .
. . .
. . .
. . .
. . .
. . .
. . .
. . .

I

[Abandoned matinee showing in the Capitol Cinema, Sunday, 8 April, feature film *Heimkehr* (*Homecoming*), starring Paula Wessely and Attila Hörbiger] The Capitol Cinema is owned by the Lenz family. Theatre manageress, also ticket seller, is their sister-in-law, Frau Schrader. The wood panelling of the boxes, the balcony, the stalls is painted ivory, red velvet seats. The lamp coverings are brown imitation pigskin. A company of soldiers from the Klus Barracks has marched up for the showing. As soon as the gong sounds, at 10 on the dot, the lights very slowly dim, Frau Schrader herself had constructed the intermediate special resistor with the projectionist. As far as film is concerned, this cinema has seen a great deal of suspense which has been prepared for by the gong, atmosphere of the house, very slow fading of the yellow-brown lights, introductory music, etc.

Now, hurled into the corner, Frau Schrader sees, just where the right-hand row of balcony seats meets the ceiling, a bit of smoky sky, a high-explosive bomb has opened up the building and smashed its way down into the cellar. Frau Schrader had wanted to check whether auditorium and toilets were completely cleared of customers after the final warning. Behind the firewall of the next building, flames flared through the drifting smoke. The devastation of the right-hand side of the cinema stood in no meaningful or dramatic relationship to the film shown. Where

was the projectionist? She ran to the cloakroom, from where she could see the imposing foyer (cut-glass swing doors), the display cases for forthcoming attractions, all 'higgledy-piggledy' in a mess. She wanted to set to work there with an air-raid protection shovel, clear up the rubble in time for the 2 p.m. screening.

This was probably the most powerful shock that the cinema had ever experienced during the time Frau Schrader was in charge, the effect triggered by even the best films is hardly comparable. For Frau Schrader, a seasoned cinema professional, however, there was no conceivable shock, which could call in question the division of the afternoon into four fixed screenings (or six with matinee and late show). But meanwhile the 4th and 5th assault waves, which dropped their bombs on the town from 11.55 a.m., approached with an unpleasant and 'low' humming sound, Frau Schrader heard the whistle and the roar of the bombs, the explosions, so she hid herself in a corner between box office and cellar entrance. She never went down to the cellar, since she didn't want to be buried under rubble. Once her eyes were more or less functioning again, she saw through the shattered glass of the little box office a string of silver machines flying off in the direction of the Deaf School.

Now she did begin to have second thoughts. She made her way over the pieces of rubble that covered Spiegelstrasse, saw that the ice-cream parlour in the corner house of Spiegelstrasse had received a direct hit, reached the corner of Harmoniestrasse, joined some men from the National Socialist Motor Corps who, with crash helmets, but without vehicles, were looking in the direction of the smoke and the fire. She reproaches herself for having abandoned the Capitol. She wanted to hurry back, but the men stopped her, as the facades of the buildings on Spiegelstrasse were expected to collapse. The houses were burning 'like torches'. She tried to find a better word for what she saw in such detail.

By late afternoon she had worked her way through to the corner of Spiegelstrasse and Hauptmann-Loeper-Strasse (she still said Kaiserstrasse); here there is a square, formed by the convergence of five streets; she stood next to the concrete pillar which hours before had borne a public clock and looked diagonally across to the Capitol Cinema, now burnt to the ground.

The Lenz family, who were staying in Marienbad at the time, had still not been informed. It was impossible, however, for the cinema manageress to get to a telephone. She circled the plot with the ruin of the cinema and from the courtyard of the neighbouring building managed to reach the cellar emergency exit. She had got hold of soldiers, who helped force a way in with pickaxes. In the cellar corridor lay some six members of the matinee audience, the pipes of the central heating had been ruptured by explosions and poured a jet of hot water onto the dead. Frau Schrader wanted to establish some order here at least, placed the boiled and scattered body parts—whether dismembered as a result of this occurrence or of explosive force—in the wash cauldrons of the laundry room. She wanted to make a report to some responsible authority, but in the course of the evening was unable to find anyone willing to accept a report.

She walked, shattered by now, all the way to the 'Long Cave' where, in the company of the Wilde family, who had fled there during the raid, she chewed a sausage sandwich and they took turns spooning preserved pears from a jar. Frau Schrader felt 'no good for anything any more'.

[Emergency deployment of a company of soldiers in the Plantage Park, too late from the start] The company, minus the six who had chosen the cellar of the Capitol, had left the cinema by the emergency exits and made its way in a column as far as the Blankenburg railway line. During the raid the men threw themselves on the ground in the gardens of the villas there. Later they received the order to march to First Aid Post I in the building of the Teachers' Seminary in the park. There they were assigned to the Plantage air-raid shelter, opposite the brick buildings of the hospitals. This public shelter had received three direct hits. So they dug up about 100 in-part terribly mutilated bodies, some out of the earth, some out of identifiable pits that had made up the shelter. Of what further use this operation was supposed to be, after excavation and sorting, was baffling. Where were the bodies to be taken? Were means of transport, perhaps, available?

Next to the shelter, standing askew, there was still the sign: 'Damage to or improper use of this public air-raid shelter will be prosecuted—The Mayor as Local Police Authority Mertens'.

A few yards from the former shelter the sections of lawn that had accumulated, when the trenches had been dug, were piled on top of one another in readiness for the time after the war. This stack, each item two hands breadth of earth and dead grass was untouched. The grass, however, was not completely dead, but since 1939 eked out a kind of meagre grass life, and, in the *postwar period*, such was the intention of the Parks Department of the time, would once again round off the outer skin of the park. It was valuable 100-year-old lawn, turf or sod in fact. Since the town administration had other worries than laying out the Plantage Park anew, the organizational basis for this resurrection was now absent. The neatly layered piles looked like coffins. To that extent they were superficially well matched with the collection of dead whom the soldiers had laid out on the remaining lawn between the fallen trees; in the eighteenth century, when they were planted, these had been the home of silk worms. It was merely a deceptive *impression*, since, of course, the piled-up remnants of lawn were quite useless as coffins.

[The Unknown Photographer] The man was apprehended by a military patrol in the neighbourhood of the Bismarck Tower/

PHOTO NO. 1 by the unknown photographer.
Fischmarkt, view of Breiter Weg, on the left Café Westkamp.

Spiegelsberge. He still had the camera in his hand, exposed films, unused film, photographic equipment were found in his jacket pockets. Close to the scene of the offence, i.e. close to the spot where he last took photographs, are the entrances to the underground facilities which have been blasted out of the rock and in which armaments production is housed.

The leader of the patrol meant to prove the guilt of the unknown person or spy without more ado, and so asked him: What have you been photographing?

The unknown person maintained that he had wanted to record from this distance the burning town, his hometown, at this moment of its misfortune. He maintained that he was owner of a camera shop on Breiter Weg, of all his equipment as a photographer he had grabbed only camera and films and managed to

PHOTO NO. 2. Martiniplan, on the left the south pier of Martinikirche Church.
In the background, the tavern Saure Schnauze ('Sour Snout').

make his way along the Fischmarkt, Martiniplan, Westendorf,
then by way of Mahndorf towards Spiegelsberge. The patrol
leader immediately draws his attention to the fact that this involves
him entering the prohibited military area of the caves. It's not at
all credible that you have come from Breiter Weg, he told the cul-
prit, because no one can have come out of the town from there.
Given the major events of the day, the patrol leader, exiled to a
relatively boring post in the woods, could not have hoped for a
better catch.

As soon as the soldiers, the prisoner in front of them, coming
along Moltkestrasse from the south, tried to get through to the
military headquarters building, they saw that the 'headquarters',
about 50 yards away behind a veil of smoke, was a heap of bricks,
bits of iron, etc. In their temporary quarters the officers seemed

PHOTO NO. 3. Entrance to Schmiedestrasse.

to find the prisoner a distraction in the performance of their duties. They took possession of the camera. The exposed films were passed on to an official vehicle.

Depending on whether proof was provided the man would have to be shot in Magdeburg. What's the point of espionage, now in April, in the hill area? asked First Lieutenant von Humboldt. It was conceivable, however, that the enemy was using very small aircraft to find the hidden cave entrances to the subterranean armaments plants.

PHOTO NO. 4. Westendorf, inhabitants fleeing the town.

The soldiers, in possession of a handwritten note on which the arrest was confirmed, led the prisoner along Richard Wagner Strasse. They hoped that in Wehrstedt some form of transport to Magdeburg really would be organized or that a passenger train going to Magdeburg was still stopping at the available railroad area, otherwise they would not have known what to do with the man. Whether the guards released the unknown person because of his protests, also persuaded to do so because of some doubts about the point of what they were doing in such devastated surroundings or whether the guards were distracted for a moment

PHOTO NO. 5 . Opposite the central post office.

by the detonation of an unexploded bomb near Heineplatz, so that he escaped, we do not know.

[Cemetery gardener Bischoff] Bischoff is driving his horse-drawn dray with four coffins on it along Gröperstrasse. The yield of the early morning: Harsleben (retired farmer, 1 bot. blackcurrant schnapps, 4 eggs); 1 corpse from Mahndorf (inspector, 1 bot. advocaat, wrapped in cloths, 2 frying sausages); 2 corpses from the District Hospital cold room, freshly operated. The cemetery gardeners have to take care of the transport themselves, since the undertaker's firm, Pietät, has no vehicles.

Because of the final warning Bischoff should have sought shelter long ago and not remained on the street, should have stopped the dray, entered one of the rickety half-timbered houses, looked for the cellar. He prefers to increase the pace,

PHOTO NO. 6. Final vantage point of the photographer.

cracks the whip round the horses' ears. Half turning, he sees the squadrons of the bomber force coming from the east. The corpses must not be overturned by the blasts. Bischoff feels himself under an obligation in two cases because of the gifts. He cannot stop the cart, tether the horses somehow and run to some cellar entry. 'Sane schänen fàre sind'n tir verjenejen'—'Such fine horses are an expensive pleasure.'

Bischoff races up Alt-Gräber Strasse to the new cemetery. There he lifts the coffins from the cart and places them one on top of the other. Then he climbs down into one of the open trenches, so that he now sees only a bit of sky above him, a blue that hurts the eyes.

Make every old year new,
Every age eat its fill.[1]

1 He says this in Low German dialect.

Earth crust trickles down from the bank of soil because of the explosions in the Middle and Lower Town. Bischoff is sleepy, he had set out early. Still no aircraft in the section of sky above him. Because of the overtime to come, he curls up (he has spread out his dirty jacket on the ground) and has a nap. So that he has something in reserve.

[The tower observers, Frau Arnold and Frau Zacke] Frau Arnold and Frau Zacke are on air-raid defence duty on the gallery of the bell tower of St Martin's Church, posted there as aircraft observers. They have made themselves at home on folding chairs, with torches, not needed during the day, with beer, packets of bread, binoculars, walkie-talkies. They came up here when the warning siren sounded, are still busy surveying the sky through their binoculars, when they see two formations, staggered in height, approaching from the south. They report: Height approx. 10,000 feet, heading towards Quedlinburger Strasse/Heineplatz,[2] B-17 long-range bombers. Smoke flares above the South Town. Frau Arnold adds, shouting into the radio set held by Frau Zacke: 'They're dropping bombs!' Twelve volleys of bombs dropped on either side of the Blankenburg railway line. Frau Arnold: Crowds of people with bag and baggage still running in the direction of Spiegelsberge. Frau Zacke: Not all the machines have dropped their load.

With that the flow of words of the tower observers is over for the moment. Both women count. They have put down the binoculars. 'Thirty-eight.' It's unclear whether aircraft or bomb loads dropped. Frau Arnold reports: Steinstrasse and Harden-

---

2 Named after the sausage-maker Heine, whose factory was at the edge of the built-up area of town, about three-quarters of a mile away from the two observers.

bergstrasse, Kühlinger Strasse, Heineplatz, Richard Wagner Strasse.

The first group has reached Wehrstedt and is circling, waiting for the main force. Headquarters checks back on the intercom: What 38? Frau Zacke replies for Frau Arnold, who is holding the radio: First 38 and 96 machines behind them. Assembling over Wehrstedt.

The tower observers are informed that over Nordhausen, 10 minutes flying time away, further waves of bombers are following. Frau Zacke replies: There are enough here! She can see that the aircraft have left their loop and are flying straight towards them from the direction of Wehrstedter Bridge/ Hindenburgstrasse, but doesn't report immediately, because she's counting, processing the impression. At an angle to these aircraft, smaller, faster machines are flying from the direction of Oschersleben, dropping smoke cones over Breites Tor, Schützenstrasse and as far as Fischmarkt. One of the twin-engine planes dives from a height of about 3,000 feet to 1,000 feet, deposits smoke cones over Gröperstrasse (i.e. far away to the north). Frau Arnold shouts into the radio: 'A thick yellow mass of yellow.' Black smoke flares over the Fischmarkt, etc., yellow over the Lower Town.

The aircraft were now flying over the observers. Over a stretch of about 1,000 yards, the whistle of the falling bomb loads. Frau Zacke shouts into the radio: Explosions Breites Tor! Masses of incendiary bombs! The tower observers cease making their reports, folding chairs, supplies have fallen in a heap. Frau Zacke warns Frau Arnold about 'storm winds' (pressure waves from the explosions). The women must hold on more firmly.

There was no point in fleeing. The women force themselves to squat down, both hands holding onto the ledge, still looking up at the aircraft, a second group approaching, at a height of about 6,500 feet. 'Kulk, Breiter Weg, Woort, Schuhstrasse, Paulsplan.' They whisper the details, reciting them just as they have been trained, but no longer pass them on. They get the impression, 'that the tower is moving'. Frau Zacke looks in the direction of the Cathedral Square, i.e. to the northwest. There, bombs are crashing down on the houses on Burggang. Frau Zacke says: 'They're working their way through the town.' The women prefer to lie flat now. Frau Arnold has her head close to the radio apparatus. What should she say into it? That at the moment she sees no possibility of getting away. Although she would very much like to get away from here. She sees the direct hit on the Town Hall.

Frau Zacke grabs the radio and zealously shouts something into it. A likeable anti-aircraft gunnery officer, who stood a bottle of Nordhauser schnapps, had told her: to pay attention to nothing else, just keep on reporting. So as long as she squats or lies here she is firmly determined to 'howl into the apparatus'. The tower observers have been given the nickname 'hyenas', because they 'howl in despair', one of their instructor's 'jokes'. Underneath the women the wooden casing inside the tower had begun to burn, also parts of the cupola. Flames 'crackle' from the tower onto the houses to the side of Martiniplan. Burning are: Café Deesen, Krebsschere Lane, the 'Sour Snout', etc.

Frau Zacke does not want to 'burn up' on the stone ledge of the tower gallery. She nudges her colleague, grabs folding chair, binoculars, walkie-talkie and runs into the tower and down the wooden stairs. Frau Arnold clatters down behind her. A powerful draught or storm wind presses the women against the railing. As they go Frau Zacke shouts into the radio: 'Church is burning. On our way.' The substructure of the stairs slips away under their running feet right through a column of flame and crashes onto the tower foundations. Frau Arnold, lying under burning beams, doesn't move, doesn't respond to the calls of Frau Zacke, whose thigh is broken. She's lying below the fire, close to the little door to the church nave, towards which she crawls, dragging the lower part of her body together with its pains behind her ('trailing'). She pulls herself up by a stone strut, so that arms and head reach the lower part of the closed door. She shouts for help, bangs on the wooden door with one hand. Unconscious for a while, after that she collects herself, bangs.

Hours pass. Frau Arnold, whom Frau Zacke can no longer see from this position, doesn't hear, gives no sign. The fire works its way, stage by stage, down the interior construction of the tower. On the rubble of stones and charred wood, which has settled on Frau Arnold, stands the bell, which has slipped out of its mounting down to the bottom of the tower. Frau Zacke feels she is being 'roasted' by the glowing mountain of wood and the bell at her back.

Essels un Apen,
das gluowet und hofft,
werd Bedde verkofft!
Muot up en Struohsack slapen.[3]

Frau Zacke doesn't have a straw bed, but holds herself upright on one leg, which goes numb, apart from that supporting herself with one arm on a stone projection. The broken thigh,

3 Low German verse: 'Donkeys and monkeys believe and hope they will both be sold! Must sleep on a bed of straw.' [Trans.]

twisted round, 'pulls her down' and that's 'a torment'. She'll have something to talk about, of course, if she gets rescued after all.

Why does no one get her (and the dead Frau Arnold, if no one knows whether she is still alive) out of this situation, after the air-raid protection organization posted them here? Frau Zacke carried out observations of raids on 11 January '44, 22 February '44, 30 May '44, but she missed 14 and 19 February '45 (Junkers plant), because the other hyena was on duty.

She finds a bar, scorched iron, which has cooled down, it must be late at night, and knocks against the door with it. Inhabitants from the houses on Martiniplan had taken shelter in the nave. They survived the collapse of the burning church roof in side chapels, and now open up to Frau Zacke, who has fallen across the threshold, pull her into the nave. Thank you so much, she says.

[The wedding in the Horse] I was here early this morning at 6 and had a look around. Didn't want you getting here and nothing prepared. Flowers and everything. It was the bride's mother who said that, as they arrived from the cathedral and saw the decorated hard-times breakfast: the battery of Harzbräu beer, 4 bottles of Moselle wine, which the hotel had set up from its reserves; the bride's side added ham, butter, 2 ring cakes.

Then at 11.20 the general warning. The war-duty waitress said: You absolutely must go down to the cellar. The wedding guests knew that themselves. They blethered their way through the door, along the corridor, down the beige-painted cellar stairs: bride (from the Lower Town), at present conscripted to Junkers, bridegroom (a heavy concrete engineer), mother of the bride, mother of the bridegroom, 4 sisters of the mother of the bride, a sister of the bride, her brother, who only came as far as the cellar door, as he was on duty as air-raid warden, so had to go outside again, four children from the bride's extended family, who had scattered flowers. Twelve minutes later they are all buried.

I hope they suffocated immediately, said the brother of the bride, searching in the mound of rubble the following day.

After the ceremony in the cathedral, which took longer, because there were two couples in front of them, the wedding party had about 40 minutes in the Horse. The brother of the bride had brought a portable gramophone and played the bride's 'favourite song':

Dream my little baby,
You will be a lady,
And I will be a wealthy cavalier.[4]

After that the mother of the bride pointed to the laid table, handed out plates. And whoever doesn't want, she said, has already had. And whoever doesn't have, responded the bridegroom mother, will get. The witnesses presented their empty plates.

Lissy should just let it be! said the mother. And if I don't hear anything from Edeltraud, I'll bear it with dignity. The bridegroom mother supports her: Just don't go there. Don't give Edeltraud an inch, and I'm not going to clean the flat, not ever, continued the mother of the bride. Not the windows either. Quite right, said the bridegroom mother.

---

4 'Träum mein kleines Baby, / du wirst eine Lady, / und ich werd ein reicher Kavalier.' Hit song from the 1930s. [Trans.]

What are you reading there? Gerda, a teacher and one of the sisters of the mother of the bride, asked the eight-year-old flower scatterer, Hanna's boy. Oh, you're reading the opera guide? That's a good idea. The boy's always reading. What's he reading then? cried the bridegroom's mother. The opera guide! In the church and now for the last few minutes the boy was reading the plot of one opera after another.

I've cleared away the wreaths. Sister Hanna is addressing a danger that could kill the mood of the day. In the bride's family there was a death only two weeks before. That's why Hanna says, took the wreaths away, and put in petunias instead. They suit the day better. I speeded it up. We're not allowed to put down gravel. But in September soil will be added again. Then that'll be gone too. A few days have passed by now anyway. She wants to lift the mood and so says Cheers. What beautiful wedding presents, says Gerda.

They wanted to be finished here by 1 p.m., then have lunch in the apartment in Gröperstrasse, coffee and cake at the bride's great-aunt, who can't walk any more. For the evening tables have been reserved at the 'Sour Snout'. The bridegroom has been ordered to Barby on the Elbe for the following day, Monday.

The newly-weds hardly talk to each other. The atmosphere is strained. That must change before an hour has gone by, the mother of the bride and the bridegroom's mother are working on it. Because there's a real risk: bridegroom comes from a property-owning family in Cologne. The Halberstadt girl, his bride, on the other hand, comes from the Lower Town, family without assets. There is as yet no real warmth between the opposing family groups (except of course between the bride and the groom who had been the cause of the whole business, but now remain silent). The bride's family hoped for a crisis-free day until the couple could be brought to their room in the Horse at 1 a.m. (or be ceded a room in the Gröperstrasse apartment, it now didn't matter which). Then they would also have ticked off this celebration. The mourning finished off beforehand in the quickest possible way. The family felt it was all too much. As already said, no one survived.

[Moles] This public air-raid shelter has room for 120 people. About 60 have come, weakly illuminated by the cellar light bulbs, sitting on garden chairs, stools, pallets, benches or on their suitcases and bags. As the 'shuddering drone' intensifies, followed by the whistle of the falling bombs, a few more people manage to run through the double doors, which are barred by the air-raid wardens. 'Explosions nearby,' says the senior warden. The light bulbs flicker, go out. We slide from our seats onto the cellar floor, find ourselves lying across the limbs of others. A crowd of cellar occupants rushes towards the double doors after the first series of explosions, they want to get out. The group of wardens throw themselves in their way. 'You are not allowed to leave the air-raid shelter during the raid.'

But now men and women with torches examined the wall for the breakthrough points. No one wants to stay in the darkness. They want to see what's happening. They come back, whisper. The double doors can't be opened. The occupants are divided into groups. Two wounded men—I later learnt that they were from the military hospital in the 'Cathedral Club' and had fled into our shelter from their Sunday walk—pushed their way forward to the wardens and led a group of women, who with pickaxes and shovels opened the breakthrough to the neighbouring cellar; behind them, in smaller groups of eight to ten persons, in a queue organized by the air-raid wardens, came our buried community. We explored the neighbouring cellar in which four bodies were lying, dead by asphyxiation. Exits blocked by rubble. Directed by the two corporals we use picks and iron bars to clear the breakthrough to house no. 64, we don't know that, but it's passed round in a whisper; in this cellar, however, we already see the mess, lit up by our torches, which hum at the pressure of a thumb. Debris also down the cellar stairs. We find the breakthrough to no. 66. In this cellar we had to search. There was no breakthrough to be found. The queue was jostling behind us. Some in the leading group could no longer raise their arms as much as at the beginning, were replaced. Is there a man or a woman with strong arms at the back there? Trude Willeke came forward, took the pickaxe. We then push shelves with homemade jam aside, also asparagus and beans, the jars fall and behind this mush the breakthrough. We come into a quite tidy, whitewashed cellar, but as soon as we had broken open the cellar door leading upwards—rubble and beams. Consequently the corporals said: We won't get through here. We remained underground, therefore, but should leave behind the baggage, which some were dragging along. After that we opened the breakthrough to the building of the Schlegelbräu Tavern. Here we see clouds of dust and smoke seeping in. The iron shutters of the cellar windows have burst open, dim light from outside. The queue led in behind us. At this moment (as we learn later) the 4th and 5th waves of the raid. We lay flat on the ground. The bottles tinkle in the side rooms. Then climbed up at the Heineplatz building, behind us about 70 people, led like a nursery class, over a peak of rubble as tall as a house, and saw Quedlinburger Strasse, strewn with lumps of debris, past the

Reserve Military Hospital, along the slaughterhouse wall. Without baggage we march through the woods and are handed over at the 'Long Cave', i.e. representatives of the SA and of the NSV (National Socialist Welfare), who are in charge here, attend to us.

As far as the bags hidden in the cellar of the house near the Schlegelbräu Tavern are concerned, when we went to look for them the next day they had disappeared. That hit us very badly. But we could find no authority on which to take revenge.

[Butter shop Henze. As soon as one can think clearly again— attempts at salvage] There are seven dead in the cellar of our house, 21 Hoher Weg. In our heedlessness we don't look back, run across debris, rubble, rubbish, etc., 'as over a rock garden, in which nothing is growing', towards Johannesbrunn, because we tell ourselves: We must get to a bigger square with wide roads in all directions to flee down. Other Halberstadters have already gathered here, that gives energy. Making a big detour we go back, down Dominikanerstrasse. The lower part of Hoher Weg is burning. We try along Lichtengraben. We succeed, this time making our way along the middle of the road on Hoher Weg. We see our house, no. 21, 40 yards away. Same as first impression (when we didn't get a look), which triggered our flight: destroyed by direct hits. The houses are burning, gale blowing, we hold on tight to each other in the middle of the road.

We have to hurry (we've been thinking that for one or two hours). We haven't noticed that a canister, from which green and sulphurously yellow phosphorus flames are spurting, is lying in the narrow passageway between the burning buildings of Gebhardt's Groceries and the corner of Lichtengraben at our back. We jump over the burning object with great leaps, get to the butter-and-cheese shop (Henze), the upper storey of which is burning. The owner is trying to rescue stock. The things are standing in part in the shop and in the ground-floor backrooms. We join the chain. Carry eggs, boxes of margarine, cheese, butter, boxes of ersatz honey onto the street. 'We're wading through cheese.' Sugar trickles out of the sacks, crunches between the trampled cheese boxes. Above all we have to get out of the rooms. 'The back rooms are collapsing.' A curtain is burning in a window to the yard, billowing towards the fire. The owner shouts: 'Here, take what you can, whatever you can carry!' We carry away the saved goods at a smart pace. On Schäfergasse large groups of bombed-out people. Here a troop of firemen is getting ready: unloading hose and hydrant equipment. Behind the line of firemen we organize a safe place for what we've salvaged: a large blanket which identifies part of the pavement as our new plot of land, a two-man guard beside it (Frieda, Gerda); we hurry back into town, appropriate a quilt which had been left lying, a box (Christmas-tree decorations), a stamp collection lying on top of a wheel-barrow, as well as a torch. I say to Willi he should remove the collection inconspicuously.

The brick building of the *Halberstadt Tageblatt* newspaper, Lichtengraben, I want to place an accommodation-wanted advert for the next few days, possibly a summer house, edge of town. We can't accept it. We're not appearing, says one of the editors. I grab pencils and ink, take them to the rest of the saved stuff in Schäfergasse. I station two children there, send Gisela, Frieda to Klein-Quenstedt, they are to say, we have lost everything and could they not let us have a ham. Really do come back with three sausages and a winter coat. Our collecting point with salvaged goods of varying quality now spreads over 12 square yards. That's in the way here, says someone from the Party, who is checking the situation here. Distribute it more to the back there, on Vogtei. However distribute it is just what we mustn't do, but keep it together. Hoses have to be laid through here, says the man in uniform. The firemen thoughtlessly lay down their hose across our property. We are full of public spirit. The children want to join in putting out the flames, but are shooed away. Now we have to think about the night, how we can somehow shelter close to our goods.

[In the editorial office] Should we bring out a newspaper or go to put out the fires? Put them out with what? They stack the paper supplies in the cellar. Someone says: It would be better if it all burnt in one place, where we can keep the fire in check. We'll save this stone building, if we manage to get everything inflammable out of the way. We cover the relief plates with damp cloths. So down with the curtains.

There are a few pails of water. One of the typesetters says: If everyone pees again, we'll have more, we should call in 'passers-by', who can be milked into a pail.

The catastrophe has now been running its course since 11.32 a.m., i.e. for almost one and a half hours, but clock time, which ticks by evenly as before the attack, and the sensory processing of time are diverging. With the brains of tomorrow they could think up practical emergency measures in these quarters of an hour. Two editors are sent to the Gate Pond, are supposed to drag over water in a large barrel, so that the cloths for the presses can be dampened. The wooden stairwell also has to get a damp covering. The white spirit and the oily printer's ink must be removed, perhaps to an inaccessible cellar corner? But what do we do with the coal there? Do we shovel it into the next yard? Better to bury it. There's a small stretch of lawn next to pear tree and wall that can be used for burying. One could also block the entry to the coal cellar with rubble and stones. But the most important thing is to deal with the paper stock.

In the yard the typesetters light controlled fires to destroy the supply of paper, in itself valuable. Meanwhile men and women of the editorial staff are standing in the attic with fire-beaters and shovelfuls of sand, ready to beat out the sparks blown among the beams or scatter sand on them. Coffee is made from the precious water. Pails and canisters from which the printer's ink has been emptied are carried to the swimming baths.

[9 Domgang] In the windows, just after the air raid, there was, knocked over, a range of tin soldiers. The remainder, 12,400 men in all, Ney's III. Corps, desperately advancing through the Russian winter towards the easternmost stragglers of the Grande Armée, was packed away in boxes in cupboards. It was set up once a year in Advent. Only Herr Gramert himself could place the mass of soldiers in the correct order. In panic-stricken flight away from this apple of his eye he has been struck on the head by a burning beam in Krebsschere Lane, is unable to make any further decisions. The apartment at 9 Domgang, with all the marks of Gramert's personal style, lies quiet and intact for another two hours, except that it grows ever hotter in the course of the afternoon. At about 5 p.m., like the tin figures in their boxes, which melt into lumps, it has burnt out.

[Zum Harder] At about 2 p.m., in this inn on the Weinmarkt, flames lick at the sign hanging behind the bar: 'No cheery fart will escape an anxious arse.' The jumbled beer glasses crack. A little later the mass of rubble of the whole house collapses onto the scorched beer counter.

II

[**Strategy from below**] Gerda Baethe, evacuated from the Gelsenkirchen district, primary-school teacher, now conscripted as munitions worker, lives with her three children, nine, seven and five, in the back house of the property at 55/57 Breiter Weg, which has no cellar. She heard the siren at 11.32 a.m., bombs exploding in the distance, she had just finished dressing the children, when bombs penetrate the air-raid shelter of the building at no. 9 (Koch's Printers), hit the building at no. 26, the house opposite, no. 69.[5]

The door of the little garden house breaks, a thick cloud of smoke and dust. 'The detonations were accompanied by an

5 Eighteen people seeking shelter suffocate in these cellars. Gerda Baethe does not know that.

extremely loud, shrill and unpleasant sound,' immediately pre-
ceded by a deep roar and a high-pitched whistle, as well as a
rising and falling drone, which Gerda, however, took to be 45 to
60 feet above her. It was, all at the same time, 'near', getting
under the protective circle, which she drew round herself and
her property. She fell to the ground, two children close to *her*, the
third ran in, collapsed on the floor. She thought: They're near.
She herself had not been hit as she lay there. The children
crawled under her, pressed against her thighs, her neck, beside
her head, tried to nestle up to larger body surfaces, the five-year-
old boy by shoving his head under his mother's body. At least
Gerda's troop was not scattered to the winds, but sought to stay
in physical contact.

It was a matter of seconds. The irregularly swelling drone
grew louder once again. The high explosive bombs penetrated
the cellar of the solid building at no. 21 (EPA Store). She 'felt' the
impact as 'at a distance of 15 feet'. The little garden house was
shaken by the pressure wave; the next series of explosions: Woort,
Kulkplatz, Paulsplan, French Church, Fischmarkt, Büttner Store,
Gothic House, etc. Gerda registered it as 'far away'. She could
not, after all, enter it or see it on any situation map. She lay on
the floor, 'the burden' of the children's bodies on and beside her,
'listened'. The children didn't move, didn't cry out. She nudged
the middle one, who immediately began to whimper. The reaction, now the two others were crying as well, confirmed that her
little ones were still active. That, seen from her little family island,
they were not yet counted among the dead.

While at some height the swelling deep hum came closer
again, Gerda struggled to her feet, pushed the children forward,
through the kitchen, where the little hanging salt, pepper, sugar,

herbs boxes had fallen down and scattered their contents across the floor tiles—the stove had fallen apart, remains of the fire on the tiles, leave it, she thought, shoved her brood down the six steps to the tool corner, which was the closest this little building had to something like a cellar. It was 5 feet below street level. She felt herself to be 'lightly armed' in her 'unequipped little house'. She did not believe there was a danger of being buried. When the bombs fell she always held her breath for a long time, held her breath till it was over, because she had heard that the pressure wave of the bombs tore the air sacs of the lungs, i.e. produced a build-up of pressure in the lungs. Now she whispered to her youngest child: Don't breathe, please don't breathe. The whispering made the child nervous. The oldest puffed out her cheeks, breathed nevertheless.

There was no time. Principles of a 'strategy from below' which Gerda tried to assemble in her mind during these seconds, could not be conveyed from here, far below, to the planners, invisible to Gerda at 10,000 feet above the town, never mind much further, to the air bases from which the bombers had started, where the senior planning staffs were to be found. The attics of the buildings on Breiter Weg burnt immediately. After a pause of about 10 minutes, during which Gerda heard a constant trickling sound, which had something to do either with the burning itself or with the 'roof tiles coming down', she looked once through the hole, in which there were still a few broken shards of glass, saw the flames in the front house, lumps of rubble in the yard; the view of the neighbouring courtyard was blocked by a high wall (it could mean shelter). Now the sound of the big aircraft swelling again. She began to curse the bombers. But if success meant one of them plunging to the ground and killing her together with the rest of her garden-house

occupants, then it would be better not to do it. She was most concerned with her youngest, because he was her little son (whereas
she believed she would be able to replace the less valuable girls
later on). She seriously weighed up which of the three would
most urgently need to be rescued, tried to draw satisfaction from
the fact that she included herself in this order of precedence: in
different positions, she was only feeling her way for the moment.
Perhaps she could do something more, by placing herself in front
of one of the children at the next pressure wave and deflecting
it from the lungs of the child, which, she still had to choose.
Admittedly she could not deflect a small house should it collapse.

Tactically, at least, it appeared promising, that with this little
garden house not too much would collapse onto her. An advan-
tage of the apartment allocation. She now crawled over the children, who were clinging to her. But that was the very thing that
suddenly made her feel afraid, and she got to her feet in order
to shake them off, noticed as she did so, that she was breathing,
and admonished herself to be careful: don't 'take in' this air,
whose pressure fluctuated under the influence of the explosions!

She forced herself to 'think' strategically, i.e. with reference
to the main points: where to flee, should an opportunity arise
once again through waiting for a next wave. She then wanted to
run across the Fischmarkt, Martiniplan, Schmiedestrasse, Westendorf. A wheel-barrow in the yard, the little ones into it and
race off to the fields or villages.

She set this comforting image at the forefront of her mind,
there was no other means of defence available to her, as the 4th
and 5th waves devastated the town centre: Schuhstrasse, Hoher
Weg, Lichtwerstrasse, etc. In addition, the rustling and clattering
of debris coming down from the roofs, or it was the sound of

fire burning. It was already starting again in the same way as 11 minutes ago, the swelling hum was growing louder. She tried to influence the trajectory of the bombs by loud praying. But if she miscalculated now? Also she didn't want to be thought a believer or superstitious, after so many years in the rational teaching profession. Outside the voices of inhabitants, who had come outside, so as not to burn in their cellars, and were discussing escape routes.

Stay lying on the floor here, said Gerda to her children. She crossed the yard: no sky, black smoke, rumbling, that was becoming more distant. Before there had been sun and blue sky.

The lovely snow white clouds drift far and wide,
I feel as though I long ago had died . . .[6]

Now clouds of thick smoke. She made her way across blocks of rubble, handcarts, stood there now, in front of the gateway of the front house, where a group of men carrying axes, wearing Air Raid Protection armbands were beginning to discuss something. She joined them, in order to get some advice. They had all had enough of this event, so that they were expecting no more waves of bombers (on this harmless town!). All behaved as if nothing else was going to happen. There is nothing to save, they said. Everyone has to run out to the west. But they themselves did not run, instead gazed out of the entry quite spellbound by the collapsing facade of no. 60, behind it a huge warehouse was burning.

Gerda had found out enough. No trustworthy strategy came from diligent waiting. She left the men to their fate, ran to the

6 From 'Feldeinsamkeit' by Hermann Allers, the original German text set to music by Johannes Brahms as well as Charles Ives. The English translation is by Henry Grafton Chapman (1860–1913). [Trans.]

garden house, did not assume that there was any point in fleeing through the fires of the town, instead soberly assessed the distance to the neighbouring houses, to the front house. She chose a slat lying in the yard, but then took a length of tin guttering, which she bent the way she needed. With it she could beat out flames if they came within 6 feet. She started in the kitchen by putting out the burning remains of the stove. The children remained hidden in the little building, i.e. in the lower part. Some tools were still there: a shovel (useful), broom (not useful), rakes (possibly useful). With the shovel she dug up earth from the reserves in the flowerbeds and heaped piles against the wall to the next yard; she wanted to throw earth on the fire if it crept closer.

She had soon put down the guttering again. Now there were no more voices to be heard from anywhere round her. The front house, all the houses on Breiter Weg were burning to the ground. She didn't want to suffocate. It wasn't the flames that threatened her, but the heat all around. But because of the modesty of the garden house allocated to her—the owners of the property had played a trick on the housing office when they claimed that this unused garden house was an apartment—there was a distance of 15 to 20 yards from the flames. She had thrown bedding and other inflammable material, which the occupants of the front house had dropped into the yard, over the wall into the next yard. Now she no longer moved in the heat, 'didn't want to roast from the inside'.

Left over strategically from the whole day was only the lack of ownership of inflammable objects of value. She would also, among other things, no longer have been able to put up curtains in the garden house, because she could not get hold of any. The children were thirsty, hungry. In the kitchen Gerda gathered up sugar mixed with salt and pepper in a wooden ladle, one couldn't even fry bread. There was no fireplace. There was plenty of fire all around. She gave them a bread rind and one to two spoonfuls of margarine and four spoonfuls each of spoiled sugar.

Addendum: In order to open up a strategic perspective, such as on 8 April, Gerda Baethe, 'well toasted', especially during the night, when the heat was at its worst, in her shelter wished to have, then since 1918, 70,000 determined teachers, all like her, would have had to teach hard for 20 years in each of the countries involved in the First World War; but also at the national level—pressure on press, government; then the young people educated in this way would have been able to seize the reins or sceptre (but reins and sceptre are not strategic weapons, there was no image for the taking of power required here). 'It's all a question of organization.'

When the West Wall was being built, Gerda had spent two wonderful weeks in the Eifel Hills with a gentleman from Organisation Todt.* This gentleman drove a convertible. That means they could race across the cool hills of the Schnee-Eifel in an open-top car, from volcanic crater to volcanic crater, virtually mountain lakes. From him she had got the expression 'All just a matter of organization.' He showed her plans, on which ships go uphill across the Alps to reach the Po Plain. That was organization as canal building, as calculated by engineers. It can be done.

* A Nazi organization responsible for major construction projects, such as the West Wall, defensive positions designed to repel any French attack. [Trans].

The entry to the Alpine bar.

[**Strategy from above**] Thus Gerda swore to herself in those moments of time shortage which, admittedly, dragged on from 11.32 forenoon through the difficult night-time hours of 8 to 9 April and into the late afternoon of the following day, but in particular between the 3rd and the 4th wave, in which she had a respite of 10 minutes, that in future she wanted to lay the foundations of such organization. Eight hundred years of strategy from below would then shatter 800 past years of strategy from above, not with a length of gutter, not with a shovel and not by mere waiting and wishing. But the past was not over yet, because at this point in time the aircraft were once again approaching over Thekenberge, Spiegelsberge (4th and 5th waves), circling over Wehrstedt, could no longer see smoke flares in the chaos and so simply headed towards the cloud of smoke of the town,

Ships sailed up through the high mountains over the passes and peaks to Italy and back. From the North Sea to the Adriatic.

BELOW: One of the locks. FURTHER UP: Tunnels. Planned ships of 1938.

going down to 6,000 feet, 'raked' over the Middle Town, fairly self-confident, as no hostile fighter defence or anti-aircraft fire could be discerned. They could neither make out any details of the town, nor did they sense the cautiously muted wishes at that moment of Gerda Baethe. They could suspect nothing, 'you sweet angels, you'.[7]

The group of bombers, about 200 aircraft, was flying towards Halberstadt from the south-west at a height of about 22,000 feet. It was followed at a distance of about 10 minutes flying time, i.e. they were now over Nordhausen, by a further 115 aircraft. The formation 'in attack order', made a traditional cavalry-like impression, but it was *calculated*, not a parade, the aircraft taking up positions, in which, if they were attacked by fighter planes, they could close up to give covering fire, and if they were shot at by anti-aircraft guns, could be spread out.

The pioneering phase of such attacks with four-engine long-distance B-17 bombers, each one a workshop, but the compact formation constituting a factory, lies 3–4 years back. The completion of the process has excluded as irrational factors which were taken account of in the pioneer phase, such as trust in God, military world of forms, strategy, internal recruitment among the air crews to ensure they are willing to attack, remarks on the special features of the target, meaning of the attack, etc.

7 Allusion to a hit song of 1938. [Trans.]

Discussion 1976, near Stockholm, OECD conference: *Post-Attack Farm Problems*, in conjunction with Sipri Yearbook, Working Group VII, whose participants have seated themselves on a terrace in the light of an Indian summer. 'Evolutionary significance' of attack procedures 'in the summer phase of 1944'.

1. Professionalization

It is not the individual combatant of Valmy, the citizen in arms (proletarian, teacher, small entrepreneur), who carries out these attacks but the trained air-war expert: analytical terminology; deductive stringency; obligation on principle to provide justification in combat reports; technical know-how; etc. Problem of the 'internal abroad' of occasional personal perception, e.g. the tidiness of the fields below; rows of houses; blocks of buildings; orderly quarters reminiscent of home; reflection on assumed high summer temperatures below when instruments up in the aircraft provide no cause for it.

2. Conventionality

The crews experience it as 'daily story of their factories'.

3. Legalism

The attack assumes no moral motive or need for explanation on the part of crew or command staffs except for a general obedience. It is not evil convictions that are punished but actions deviating from the norm, e.g. turning back prematurely; undisciplined or ragged release of bombs. Legalism in particular insofar as targets indicated as secondary are not approached and bombed before higher-listed targets. *In a sense, justice lies in the flight route.*

Universality

By 1942, *effectiveness within the generalized totality* of all fighting units has replaced *thymos* (bravery) or discipline, these being *personal* characteristics and hence, with reference to the system, *limited*. It is not individual fighters or military units but the levels of the theatres of war, the Asian, the 8th Air Force, the advancing Soviet units, the lead tanks, which, on 8 April 1945, reach the southern edge of the Harz Mountains, the Marine Corps, which are in competition and reciprocal discipline, mediated by the instrumental ancillary system of the public relations departments of the Allied homelands. With that, quotes F, 'the systemic threshold to a universalist system in place of a narrowly personal one has been crossed.'

'Glows as once star by star—the isle faded and the swans.'* The lake, with no islands, lies before them, 90 feet below the rocky terrace. The participants are convinced of the incompatibility of their points of view. They look down at the lake, would like to go swimming.

* Lines from 'Schäfers Abschied' (Shepherd's Leavetaking) by Karl Kraus.

Since the pioneering phase of '42/43 cannot be ignored, without which the present raid would also not have taken place, there is a strategic residue. At that time the standard was set by lines of thought deriving from Trenchard,[8] who had experience of Verdun, and had himself begun his career in the cavalry, which goes as far back as Hannibal. The latter revives what had

8 Hugh Trenchard, Air Vice Marshal, founder and commander of the Royal Air Force in the First World War. From 1942, the US air force in the European theatre quickly learnt all it could from his ideas.

motivated early tree-climbers in the history of the species to find the nourishing amnion eggs of large dinosaurs, to bite the shell open from the side or from below and either to place their own brood inside or suck them dry. It is quite clear, that this root of strategic interest, booty, does not apply in the case of bomber crews, since they put something into the town that is their target, will never take away something from it, 'in order, even in the most abstract sense, to suck something out'. They cannot 'want to have' something here, are self-sufficient, as far as fuel and material to be dropped is concerned. At most it could be interpreted like this, that they are sucking in the labour power of the engineers in the aircraft plants back home or the oil of Texas or Arabia or that the crews are drawing pay on their private accounts or that the total transaction produces profits for the armaments companies. But the crews of the aircraft would not be sufficiently or willingly active for any of these processes. Nor at this point in time are they defending their homes or homeland. To that extent, the raw material out of which strategy is produced is meanwhile entirely absent.[9]

9 Here in particular, says Fritszche, of Working Group VII, no classes are fighting each other, no more than they were at Verdun. Instead, 'above' and 'below', *labour power* and *relation of production* are mingled altogether opaquely. The sky is clear, the singleness of purpose of the formations approaching the target, the tension between the ordinary crew members, usually from the lower classes, and elite commanders, or the whole exhausted situation of those below in the town exposed to the production relation air raid, all these are deceptive, in that, it would be necessary to work back through the generational chains in order to analyse, in an extremely complicated way, the *roots* of this whole. Yet only such an analysis would reach the *raw material* from which strategy is made, either, following Clausewitz, 'love of fatherland' or a class-specific reason, etc. To that extent, says Fritszche, one can only say that the scrap of long-past class struggles or feelings or labour power organizes itself in the *form* of this event.

　　With that Fritzsche stirs up a hornet's nest. The theme of *formality* or *procedure* takes hold of the discussion group. At first, none of the participants knows

ABOVE: The Planner.
BELOW: 'The Boys'.

what is meant by it. At any rate, there is a *formalism* involved in flying to the target and bombing it, in the gradual clearing out of burdensome real ballast as of personal motivation, moral condemnation of what is to be bombed ('morale bombing'), in calculated know-how, of automation, of looking and seeing, which is replaced by radar-guided flight, etc. Here, the aircraft are not flying in the same sense as during the Battle of Britain; instead, a conceptual system is flying, a system of ideas wrapped in metal. Willi B. is desperate to makes a link to Plato's *Phaedrus*: 'That before their birth the souls of men joined in the gladdening procession of the gods across the heavens [. . .] the souls owe their ability to cross the heavens with the gods to their plumage [. . .] they lose their plumage, plunge down and enter into union with an earthly body, in birth [. . .] the soul celebrates its origin, the images seen earlier [. . .] the coming together of souls and ideas as transition of the soul shared with the gods' (Ernst K. Specht, 'Die psychoanalytische Theorie der Verliebtheit—und Platon', *Psyche* 31(2) (1977): 106. 'And what are you trying to get at with that now, Willi?' asks Ursula D. No one knows. But the forms must come from somewhere.

STAGGERED* BATTLE FORMATION WITH ADDITIONAL AIRCRAFT FLYING AHEAD

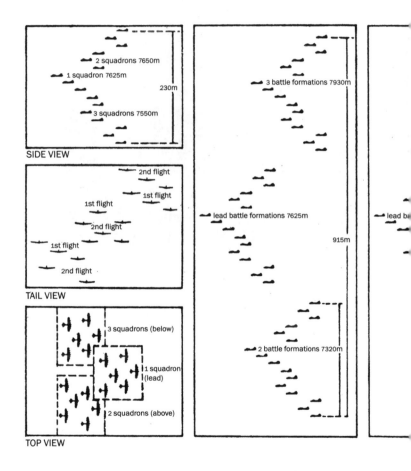

* In the 92nd, 305th, 306th and 351st groups, the crews are veterans who have already attacked Schweinfurt and Regensburg in 1943. They are day-attack specialists.

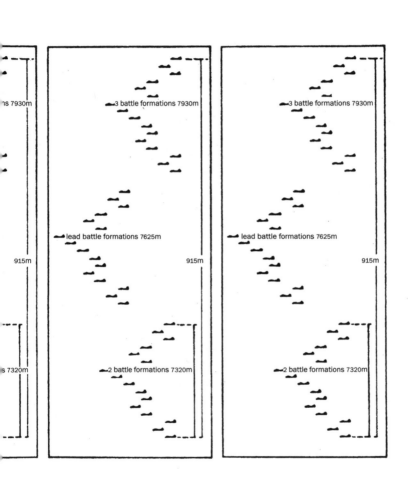

ns 7930m

3 battle formations 7930m

3 battle formations 7930m

lead battle formations 7625m

lead battle formations 7625m

915m

915m

915m

s 7320m

2 battle formations 7320m

2 battle formations 7320m

At any rate, amid the noise of the engines and because of the overpowering brightness of the daylight, it was impossible to read crime novels or pulp novels in these airborne industrial plants, although for those who were not at the controls, keeping a lookout or operating the radios, long periods of waiting had to be endured. An adaptation to the machines, simply because these were working. I imitate the walk, the facial movements, the expression of my mother, I imitate the manner of expression of society, have a nose like a car bonnet, the straightness of the roads, the rectangular shape of our houses and rooms, I imitate the engines, which draw our 'souls' behind them as appendages together with bomb load, machinery, interior fittings.

Hence none of the long-serving professionals in the aircraft can avoid the tension, turn the soul away to the fields below or the Harz Mountains or to the deep blue of the heavens.

The 8th Air Force, US Army Air Forces, made plans to attack targets in the vicinity of Berlin on 8. 4. 1945.[*] These targets were, however, within the Russian bomb line and could not be attacked by US forces without prior clearance from Russian authorities. When such clearance was not received, the 8th Air Force put in effect an alternative plan to use 25 groups of B-17s and 7 groups of B-24s for attacks on other targets in Germany.

Two of the targets selected for bombing were an airfield at Zerbst and an oil-storage depot at Stassfurt. Both these objects were to be attacked visually. If they were obscured by clouds, the planes were to bomb the marshalling yard at Halberstadt,[†] attacking either visually or by use of radar sightings.

Consequently, these groups went to their alternative object at Halberstadt. Because of 3/10 cloud cover at Halberstadt, many of the bombs were dropped by instrument sighting of the objective but some crews bombed visually.[††]

* Extracts from a letter of 29 March 1965 from the Aerospace Studies Institute to the Halberstadt historian Werner Hartmann: 'Target reserve': Ten specifically chosen target areas. Six of them for the RAF, four USAF, including the areas Stendal—Erfurt—Halle—Leipzig—Chemnitz—Magdeburg. On 8 April, out of these there was a remaining target stock. (Remaining target reserve.) By 8 April, SACEUR Order of 4 April '45, to cease area bombing, had not yet come down the chain of command to the operational airfields.

† Sixty-four thousand inhabitants. Unlike other towns which by 1939, thanks to the initiative of ambitious mayors, had expanded past the 100,000-inhabitant mark through incorporation of surrounding settlements and so were towards the top of the bombing lists, Halberstadt had not been enlarged. To the south of the town, an airfield, plants of the Junkers Company specializing in wing construction. In the mountains, towards Langenstein, shafts driven 15 miles into the hillsides for armaments manufacture. All of it, however, clearly distinct from the town. Only the Cathedral Grammar School has been emptied of pupils and teachers. An armaments staff of the Speer Ministry has been quartered there. Halberstadt is low down on the bombing lists of the 8th US Air Force, below Nordhausen, but above Quedlinburg or Aschsersleben.

†† In their machinery, the crews were, for 'psychological' reasons, blind. It is quite certain that over both Zerbst and Stassfurt, as over Halberstadt, there was an early-summer blue sky. So no clouds over Stassfurt, nor 3/10 cloud cover over Halberstadt. That the majority of the aircraft nevertheless did not bomb visually but with radar demonstrates the characteristic of eyes as strategy and not as personal organs of the relevant navigator. On the other hand, USAF Colonel Douglas (retd), 10. 4. 1977: 'I don't want to hear the word "strategy".' 'We use it,' objects one of the scholars, 'because you were called or are still called Strategic Bomber Command.' 'Twaddle,' said the colonel, 'You have to the think of it as a normal day shift in a factory.' 'Two hundred middling-sized industrial plants fly towards the town.' The scholars, however, said, 'They flew as if they were blindfolded. How can that be explained?' The colonel (retd) didn't know the answer either.

They hovered up above, with repulsive (or general) 'intelligence' they bombed the corner houses in order to block the streets to fleeing inhabitants with mountains of rubble, the inhabitants fleeing, because driven from their houses by incendiaries and phosphorus canisters. The bomber crews were, therefore (in carrying out the plans of their strategists and air-force tacticians and without adding too much will of their own), to 'downright torture' the population of the town.

As he flies over the last two mountain ridges Braddock in the lead plane of the first combat block sees a long tree-lined road crossed by a railway line. Inhabitants of the town are hurrying along this avenue with junk, handcarts towards the mountain forest. It is known from the attack files that caves have been enlarged to serve as shelters there. Braddock orders the six aircraft following him to drop one stick of bombs each on this target, since it is available. This is one of the few 'personal' decisions made within the time frame of the attack as a whole.

'Because each bomb type has a particular task to fulfil. Mines expose the combustible interiors of the buildings.' Heavy high-explosive bombs, which tear open the streets and destroy the water pipes so that fires cannot be put out in the initial stages. The smaller explosive bombs drive the fire-brigade units back into the cellars. (Air Marshal Harris: 'The first wave is flown in order to exhaust the fire services and the possibilities of extinguishing the fires.') These are followed by incendiary bombs, in particular so-called Super-flamers. From information provided by Cathedral architect W. Bolze, Cathedral Works Department, Halberstadt—this is synthetic lava made up of petrol, rubber, viscose plus magnesium. According to Harris, the sequence represents a systematic whole.

ABOVE: Ira C. Eaker (formerly Second-in-Command, 8th Air Force) left, and General Carl Spaatz (Commander, Strategic Air Forces), right.

BELOW: B. Dampson, target-marker.

THE MERCHANDISE

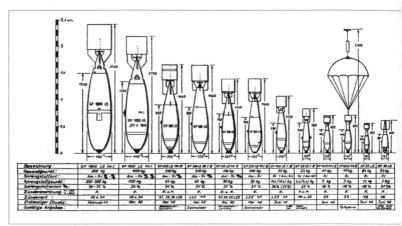

GP = General purpose bombs. HEF = High-explosive fragmentation bombs

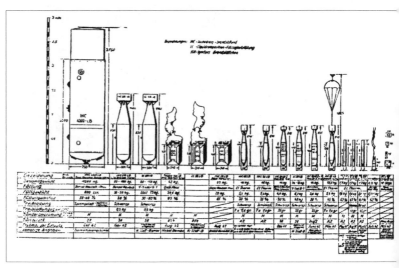

Incendiary merchandise

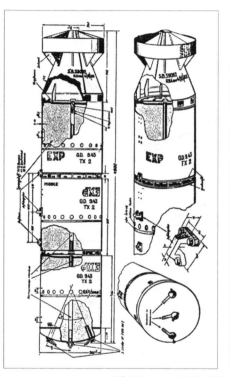
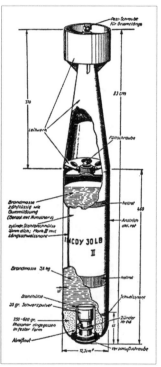

LEFT: HC (high capacity) 12,000-pound Blockbuster.

RIGHT: Liquid incendiary bomb INC 30-pound MK-IV, 'with long weld seams'.

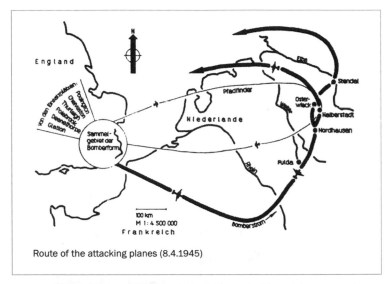

Route of the attacking planes (8.4.1945)

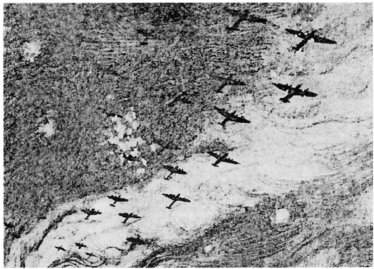

[Interview with Brigadier Anderson]

Kunzert, a reporter and native of Halberstadt, had made his way to the west with the British troops who evacuated Saxony-Anhalt in June 1945. In 1952, in London, on the fringes of a Strategic Research conference, he buttonholed Brigadier Wesley C. Anderson, formerly 8th US Air Force. They sit on barstools in the *Strand* Hotel. As a commander Anderson had been partly responsible for the attack on Halberstadt.

REPORTER. So you took off after breakfast?

ANDERSON. That's right. Ham and eggs, coffee. I always read detective stories for the passages in which the detective demolishes four plates of ham and eggs and three cups of coffee. That gives me a feeling of substance. I wouldn't eat it myself. But I like to imagine it. Joking aside.

REPORTER. Well. You took off routinely from airfields in the south of England?

ANDERSON. 92 Group, Podington. 305 Group, Chelveston. 306 Group, Thurleigh. 351 Group, Polebrook. 401 Group, Deenethorpe and 457 Group Glatton. That's definite.

REPORTER. If you don't make a list, but picture it. What does one see?

Anderson was unable to convey a clear picture. First of all, one doesn't see the listed groups; Anderson stands behind the pilot of an aircraft, sees field and hangars 'whirl past' at the side, is pressed against the rear wall, etc. He knows only from a stack of telexes (his hands suggest a pile more than a foot high), that the other groups are starting at other places at the same time. There are between 12 and 18 men (including ground crew) at work in and on each of these aircraft, some waiting, while some have to carry out specific technical movements. The sum of industrial plants, which have started, assembles, the planes circle over the south coast of England.

REPORTER. Approach path over the coast of the north of France?

ANDERSON. As usual. We acted as if we were heading for Nürnberg or Schweinfurt.

REPORTER. Does one feel proud when one looks out over a fleet of over 300 bombers?

ANDERSON. I was sitting in a Mosquito. Because of the telexes I mentioned as well as the map (and making the assumption that everything is going to plan) I could imagine this bomber stream. I couldn't see it. My Mosquito, a fast bomber, made of wood, was flying a long way from the mass of planes— Dutch coast, Rhine, Weser, Northern Harz, etc.

REPORTER. Then the air surveillance on our side would only have had to follow the pathfinder plane in order to see through the trick with the initial orientation of the bomber fleet to the south-east?

ANDERSON. Sure. To the extent that it still existed, the people there certainly saw through it.

REPORTER. Change of course south of Fulda?

ANDERSON. Course north-east.

REPORTER. As planned?

ANDERSON. It's all planned.

REPORTER. The unit commanders can't make any decisions?

ANDERSON. The lead planes fly at the front, but they don't lead.

REPORTER. Could you describe what that meant?

ANDERSON. I can't tell you what that meant. I can only say something about the method of attack. These are experts, after all. First of all they have to 'see' the town somehow. So we arrive, i.e. we Mosquitos first of all see the fleet of bombers, approaching from the south. Then the Harz Mountains are to the right, the Brocken is visible. The bombers fly over the southern part of the town, once over the whole thing, drop a couple of sticks of bombs prophy-lactically at the points where the inhabitants, warned by the sirens, are fleeing towards the hilly terrain. To close that off. The bombers then assemble at the north-east exit of the town, i.e. over the main road to Magdeburg. There are two holding patterns, so that all the aircraft are in position and the attack can be flown compactly. Carpet-bombing had been ordered, i.e. *concentration* of the bombs dropped, either on the southern or the middle part of the town. We didn't know the place, after all, only had the map and a first impression. This impression told us: the principal lines of communication run through middle and south in west–east direction, whereas there are villages to the north and moun-tains to the south. We can't spend too much time thinking about the individual town, since we still have the attack to carry out and the flight back. Question: Fighter defence, anti-aircraft fire, quality control of the bombs dropped? We don't have time to think about the layout of the town, we look for the key points.

REPORTER. What appear to you as key points?

ANDERSON. We can't know what the attack is supposed to do at this point in the war. So we choose a *reasonable* line of attack.

REPORTER. What's that?

ANDERSON. So that the attack isn't frittered away.

REPORTER. What does that mean?

ANDERSON. The bombs must not be scattered across the area of the town. So we see main roads, arterial roads. That's where a fire can really get going. You know as well as I do, where that is in an old town. We don't conduct mediaeval studies, but we've also heard that such a town dates from the year 800. That means the bombardiers have to concentrate on the corner houses first. That's how we block the road. In the best of cases: piles of rubble at the entry and exit of every street. The trap is sprung, when we open up the houses on both sides of the street with high explosive. Then into that incendiary canisters and small incendiary bombs, etc. On top of that 3rd and 4th waves, again high explosive and incendiary. That produces a vertical grid, even though we are always ploughing the same furrow. You see, it's hard to get intact buildings to burn. The roofs have to be got rid of first, and explosive bombs have to create openings down as far as the first floor or the ground floor if possible, where the combustible material is. Otherwise we don't have any extensive fires, no fire storm, etc. My brother is an air-force medic. It's just the same with the extensive treatment of a wound. A closed encrusted wound won't heal, it's a bit like an encrusted town, grown over the centuries, the wound has first of all to be torn open again, so that fresh blood vessels can set to work, and then thick ointment and gauze on top.

REPORTER. After the first four waves you started again with two further waves in flypast formation and continued the 'treatment'. Why that?

ANDERSON. Like a flypast because there was no anti-aircraft fire to be seen. With anti-aircraft fire the aircraft formation becomes ragged. Consequence—the bombs dropped are not concentrated. That was not the case here.

REPORTER. I mean, after the devastation, why go over the same place with another two waves?

ANDERSON. That was standard.

REPORTER. There are rumours. At half past nine in the morning the defence headquarters of the town is supposed to have been called from Hildesheim by an American colonel using the normal telephone network: Surrender the town, remove the anti-tank obstacles! The mayor was not present, however. The Party district leader, Detering, present in his function as Defence Commissioner, rejected the request. Thereupon the bombing took place. It is said, that if the mayor had got up earlier and had accepted the request, the town would have avoided the attack. If by 11 a.m. a large white flag had been raised on the left-hand tower of St Martin's Church (on the left, seen from the south) then the bomber squadrons would have turned round again. A woman is said to have tried to bring a white cloth sewn together from four sheets to the town headquarters or to the church.

ANDERSON. That's all folderol. At that time the bombers could no longer have been reached from a command post in Hildesheim.

REPORTER. But is there anything to the rumour?

ANDERSON. Nothing at all. The colonel would have had to make a phone call. Going through divisional staff, army staff, army group, then by way of General Headquarters in Reims to London, there by way of a connecting link to Bomber Command, back to 8th Air Force, then to the switchboards of the airfields in the south of England (at the same time, you would still have to find out which squadrons took off for which targets, that's secret, any spy could make a phone call), then an appropriate order would have had to be encoded and so on, altogether a matter of six to eight hours.

REPORTER. What would your pathfinder planes have done, the ones that dropped the smoke flares, if an easily visible big white flag made out of six sheets had been placed on the towers of St Martin's Church?

ANDERSON. That's a big piece of machinery that is flying towards the town. Not an individual lead plane. What does the big white sheet mean? A trick? Nothing at all? One might have talked about it. The following machines are coming up behind. Let's accept there are no smoke flares, then one assumes that it's not been done and either drops new ones or proceeds visually.

REPORTER. But internationally a big white flag means capitulation. 'We surrender.'

ANDERSON. To planes? Let's just play it through. A plane lands on the nearby airfield of the town—the runway, however, would be too short for a four-engine aircraft—and occupies the place with an 8- or 10-man crew? How does one know whether the person who raised the white flag has not long ago been shot by a firing squad for defeatism?

REPORTER. But that's not a fair chance. What else could the town do to capitulate?

ANDERSON. What else do you want? Don't you understand, that it's dangerous to turn back home with a volatile cargo of 4 or 5 tonnes of high-explosive and incendiary bombs?

REPORTER. You could drop the bombs somewhere else.

ANDERSON. In a forest and so on. Before the return flight. Let's assume the formations are attacked on the way back, there were still fighters available at Hanover airfield. We were actually waiting the whole time for them to take off. Who would want to take on the responsibility for the heavily laden lame ducks, just because there was a white flag somewhere? The merchandise had to be dropped on the town. It's expensive stuff. And you can't drop it on the hills or the open country after it's been produced with so much labour power at home. What, in your opinion, should be in the success report which has to go to the senior commanders?

REPORTER. You could drop at least a part on open country. Or in a river.

ANDERSON. These valuable bombs? It will never remain secret. It's seen by 215 times 8 to 10 men. Besides the town didn't mean anything to us. We didn't know anyone there. Why should someone take part in a conspiracy for *their* benefit? I would be willing to give a firing squad the order, everyone take cover, aircraft approaching from the left, and tell the prisoner he should clear off, provided that everyone keeps quiet. But that's practically never the case. So something like it doesn't happen.

REPORTER. So the town was wiped out as soon as the planning started?

ANDERSON. I would put it like this: even if a couple of particularly keen commanders of our tank columns had reached the town by 11.30 a.m. thanks to a very brilliant push by way of Goslar, Vienenburg, Wernigerode, that would not have made any difference to the system of our attack.

REPORTER. But they would have set up aircraft-warning lights, fired identifying signals next to the smoke flares.

ANDERSON. An enemy ruse!

REPORTER. You would have calmly bombed your own troops to smithereens?

ANDERSON. Not 'calmly', but 'with doubts'. There would have been radio communication between planes and perhaps that would have spoiled the concentration of the carpet-bombing. But our men weren't magicians, thank God.

REPORTER. Did you have an idea what the attack was supposed to achieve?

ANDERSON. Like I already said, not a very clear one.

REPORTER. You're cynical.

ANDERSON. Just not a hypocrite. What good does it do you if I express my sympathy now?

REPORTER. None at all.

Some ill feeling had now developed between the two. The reporter refused to let Anderson buy him a coffee, although the latter did try to win him over, because now a quite different peacetime situation existed. But nor was real hate a possibility here on the bar stools of the *Strand* Hotel.

[A correspondent of *Neue Zürcher Zeitung* [NZZ] interviews a senior staff officer] On 8 April 1945, Brigadier General William B. Roberts, a senior officer on the staff of Lieutenant General Jimmy Doolittle, is on board the plane of Captain William Baultrisius; the aircraft bears the name *The Joker*. Roberts is present as an observer, he stands behind the captain at the flight controls. Baultrisius, formerly a sailor, likes to talk. Wilfried Keller, London correspondent of the Swiss NZZ, is also on this flight, without approval from a higher authority, but having signed a declaration that for the duration of the mission he relinquishes his neutral status and is aware of the risks.

ROBERTS *(jovially)*. Look, the fields are all rectangular. The main road is straight and the rows of houses there in the town either rectangular and the blocks . . .

NZZ. But the town as a whole is not rectangular but frays away into the open country.

ROBERTS That's noticeable.

Baultrisius was an expert in gruesome stories. 'The tiny fighter plane was coming at me head-on. Sergeant Douglas fired a tracer straight at it from the front-ball turret and we were so preoccupied that we didn't notice that there was no one in the plane any more who could change course. The fighter struck the front of the B-17, ripped along the whole of the bottom. The engine block, which had separated from the fuselage of the one-seater, broke through our tail and, its propeller still turning, fell slowly down behind us. I had managed to squeeze myself to the side so I was able to bring the empty

> shell—I mean, I was the only one left—to Africa using the intact outer engines. Landed late at night. There was cold beer from Detroit.'

A little more than a mile ahead of the bomber stream are the two-engine light bombers, the wood-built Mosquitos, the 'pathfinders': the plane of the master bomber, the 'assistant machine', the meteorological plane. The fleet of bombers has meanwhile descended to attack height, i.e. about 10,000 feet. The meteorological plane receives the order to ascend to this attack height and to measure the wind speed. The assistant plane dives to 3,000 feet, drops smoke flares. One of these flares comes down in the wrong place. It's in the north of the town, far away from the others. The marker bomber himself dives to a height of 3,000 feet, above this little cloud, half sits on it. That means: 'this smoke flare is to be ignored'.

NZZ. You were telling me all about the Junkers plants. But if we keep flying on this route we're going to leave them behind on one side. So what about them?

ROBERTS. I'd thought the attack would end up more to the south. We're now flying towards the smoke flares that have been dropped. First the planes assemble there (*points to the north-east edge of the town, roughly the main road to Magdeburg*).

NZZ. So the town centre, after all.

ROBERTS. I'm sorry. It'll be morale bombing. I would have liked to show you a daytime attack on an industrial target.

NZZ. Do you bomb for moral reasons or do you bomb morale?

ROBERTS. We bomb morale. The spirit of resistance must be removed from the given population by the destruction of the town.

NZZ. But the doctrine is supposed to have been given up in the meantime?

ROBERTS. Sure. That's why I'm a bit surprised myself. You can't hit this morale with bombs. Morale is evidently not situated in the heads or here (*points to the solar plexus*), but is to be found somewhere between the persons or populations of the various towns. That's been researched and is well known at staff headquarters.

NZZ. But that has no effect on this raid.

ROBERTS. I could say: unfortunately, because our most recent findings are a victory over theology. There is evidently nothing at all in heart or head. That's anyway plausible. Because those people who are smashed to pieces don't think or feel anything. And those who, despite all the measures taken, escape the attack evidently don't bear the impressions of the disaster with them. They take all kinds of baggage with them, but it seems they leave the impressions of the moments of the attack behind.

NZZ. Such an attack, or so I imagine, for example, if I think of Zürich, at least has the value of a 'phenomenon'. The 'spirit speaks from the burning bush', one might say.

ROBERTS. Not at all. There is no more powerful *real* pressure than the one we impose for 20 minutes on such a town. I do think that, at the moment of the attack itself, people say: We'll give our morale away, our will to hold out and so on. But what do they say the next day? When a couple of miles from the burnt-down town daily routine evidently continues?

NZZ. I only wanted to know what you think about it.

ROBERTS. As an officer or a historian?

NZZ. More privately.

ROBERTS. And do you know now?

NZZ. Did I forget a question?

[**Previous day, Sunday, 7 April, 5 p.m.**] For Karl Wilhelm von Schroers[10] there always had to be as much happening as possible. He was a booty hunter, as far as terrors powerfully affecting the senses are concerned. They open up horizons. Opening up horizons means something like powerful innovations, being active outside police regulation, disaster prevention, overturning the rectangularity of all circumstances, finding and saving someone and thereby bringing along something for oneself, e.g. car and trailer full of booty, which in turn is delivered to someone else, and then making yet another person happy with the reward, causing the latter to give up desired objects and so on.

The wheat it grows with force.[11]

Karl Wilhelm parks the requisitioned DKW car beside the haystack, sees two feverish prisoners laid out in front of the barn, observed from a distance of several yards by reservists. The reservists have dug a pit beside the wretched prisoners into which the latter relieve themselves. After a brief examination von Schroers has come to a conclusion: It's something serious. They appear to be typhus cases.

---

10 Cathedral Grammar School. Leaves school at 16 with wartime-leaving certificate; takes part in 1940 campaign against Belgium and France; wounded; winter 1941 caught in the Rzhev Salient; hospitalization, thanks to the influence of his uncle, a surgeon general in the Black Forest. Now, after convalescence, is army doctor at Halberstadt Reserve Military Hospital, responsible for medical care in all the prison camps in the town: Elysium (mixed nationalities), Feldscheune, Sargstädter Weg (British POWs).

11 Line from a summer hymn by Paul Gerhardt (1607–76).

They have to remain outside here for the night. We don't have any separate compartments inside, he said. No, reply the reservists. That would not be particularly good for the sick men.

It's also not good for the old bones of the reservists to stand guard out here at night.

It has to be reported to the district medical officer for a decision. But please make it urgent, says one of the reservists. In the meantime, says Schroers, it's enough if at night one of you takes a look from time to time to see that they're still lying there. They can't escape in that condition. Yes, that's what we'll do. And, orders von Schroers, put boards round the pit, so it's not so exposed.—Yes, sir.

It's an important matter. In addition at that moment a very sharp bang. Black cloud of an explosion from the direction of the main railway station, to which von Schroers immediately feels himself drawn. There has already been an uninterrupted air-raid warning for one and a half hours.

In just such cases special powers apply. Von Schroers has the authority to rush through the town, ignoring oncoming traffic, to drive on under the dangerous sky: army doctor going into action. Experts, rescue squads stand round the perimeter of the area of destruction at the main railway station/railway repair sheds. He goes to the Station Hotel, telephones for additional rescue vehicles. A little later he's talking on the phone to District Medical Officer Dr Meyer, a grey-haired spiteful little man, to whom he passes on the news of the two suspected cases of typhus and a first-hand report of the disaster at the railway yard, a munitions train has been shot up by fighter-bombers. It's up the spout, he says. Wounded or dead?—Yes. Enough. The land-lord of the station hotel, the all-clear now, shoves a large glass of *Fassbrause* over to him; it looks like beer, but tingles like lemonade, and tastes of apple juice.

A town full of provisions. It's the catastrophic wound at the enclosed railway yards that really makes one aware how intact it is. Six ME-109 fighters fly low in a sky empty of foes. Everywhere in the town the windows are opened as a precaution, so that they don't shatter when there are more distant explosions, intact telephone network, the subordinate Party organizations going about their duties, officers of the Luftwaffe and from the infantry barracks taking a look at the railway station area—all intact, an abundance; now at 6 p.m., when muscle power and circulation are at their most active, one could practice a 100-metre or a 3,000-metre run or jump into the pool of the open-air baths. Von Schroer's trait, always to be more curious than afraid, is not the result of a lack of imagination. Admittedly his eyes see only this inn, a bit of the Wehrstedt Bridge, nothing of the destroyed railway tracks, perhaps a few houses as well, but he imagines the whole town. He did not yet know, that this was the last time he would consciously look at the intact town. If he had, then perhaps he would have taken in more. Come to the Town Hall around 11 tomorrow morning. I'll be at the town-defence headquarters. You can report the suspect cases to me then, says District Medical Officer Meyer. The latter tends to ward off new information that might mean work. Von Schroers concludes from the order that the defence headquarters of the town, as its called, appear to be permanently manned. The town is preparing for a 'final battle'. There will be some fine terrors lurking there.

[8 April, 11.29 a.m., defence headquarters of the town, Town Hall, Hinter der Münze entrance] Von Schroers gets there quite early.

Runs down stairs supported by concrete columns to the defence headquarters.

He had imagined the headquarters itself to have more technical equipment. The green-painted cellar room, mediaeval arched vaulting, is in part a telephone switchboard; also a map table, and a corner with a standard lamp and easy chairs, in which are sitting: Detering,[12] Rauchhaus,[13] Kreinach,[14] Mertens,[15] Wurtinger.[16] District Medical Officer Dr Meyer rushes towards von Schroers. Meyer is spritely, small of stature 'like a Roman', and he has a steel helmet on his grey hair. He has just managed to get through, he shouts agitatedly, the town is being attacked. What's happening outside?

That's practically impossible to ignore. Roof-spotters are speaking from loudspeakers fixed to the corners of the walls. *The officials responsible for the defence of the town* have jumped up from their chairs, stand round the map table.

Take that thing off, says von Schroers to the district medical officer. It won't help you if the ceiling comes down. You're much safer if you stand here at the door, where the arch protects you. That's the only thing that will remain standing, if the ceiling comes down. The district medical officer replies: You wanted to talk about the suspect typhus cases. Aside from that, in your opinion is it an attack on individual targets or on the whole

12 District Party chief, defence commissioner of the town and in charge of emergency services.

13 Town Party chief, leader of the local National Socialist Motor Vehicle Corps, the Party's Air Raid Protection officer.

14 SA commander, staff assistant to Chief of Operations Detering.

15 Mayor, head of the local police authority, head of Air Raid Protection, etc., specialist in administrative law.

16 Colonel, senior commander of the Halberstadt garrison.

town? Meyer removes the helmet, exposing the tousled grey hair, places himself obediently exactly under the arch of the doorway, quite an amount of 500-year-old stone above him. Give me your report on the alleged typhus cases, he insists. Von Schroers thinks that this is not the moment for such a conversation. He's annoyed that Meyer appears to be suggesting that his diagnosis of the previous day is exaggerated. For now events themselves are inclining to exaggeration, are tending to disregard Meyer's attitude of cautious denial.

Von Schroers is unable to endure the lack of news down here, leaves the protective double doors to the cellar steps open, hurries up the stairs and sees: Renaissance oriel of the Town Hall, flower boxes, containing four rows of fuchsias, sagging downwards, the orderly mass of silver-gleaming enemy aircraft, flying towards the town from Wehrstedt. Smoke markers almost directly above him. Von Schroers turns back towards the cellar.

A series of explosions nearby. The cross vaulting in the eastern part of the cellar opens up, has a hole in it. From von Schroers' position one can see smoke and sky, a jagged opening. Meyer, still standing in the doorway, grabs at von Schroers. Von Schroers finds it impossible to believe that he can be hit, he is so thirsty for knowledge and life. Mertens, Detering, Wurtinger, their assistants, who only a moment ago were lying on the floor, have come to a decision, push through the open double doors with the telephonists. In the middle of the raid the air-defence headquarters are moved to the alternative headquarters in the Hephata Home of the Protestant Church Welfare Service in Wasserturmstrasse. Von Schroers gets the information from a telephonist. He is certain that nothing can be defended from the new position either.

[Telephone call from a senior officer of the OKW = Oberkommando der Wehrmacht = Armed Forces High Command]

With a 'flash' call, i.e. one classified as of extreme urgency, then later when that wasn't much use, as a 'command conversation', Staff Colonel Kuhlake got through to Magdeburg, then the attempts to get a connection led him into the local telephone networks of Croppenstedt, Gröningen, Emersleben, Schwanebeck, back again to Genthin, Oschersleben; too far south: Quedlinburg. Halberstadt telephone exchange was not working. The colonel gave orders that troops should be deployed from Oschersleben to check on the situation. They were perhaps approaching Wehrstedt. He got that far with the civilian networks. The military connections were intact as far as Quedlinburg. The colonel had still not found out any more than that there had been a terror attack on Halberstadt. But he knew that from the air-situation reports.

The telephonist in Klein-Quenstedt spoke of a 'mushroom cloud over the town'. He could not provide information on the height and breadth of the cloud. Should he hold a ruler up against the window?

Colonel Kuhlake wanted to know whether 14 Lindenweg was still standing. He persuaded a farmer who had a property on the edge of Quedlinburg, to harness his horses and set out in the direction of Halberstadt. Landowner Dr Arnold in Mahndorf, attacked over the telephone by Kuhlake, was prepared to step outside the door of his manor house and keep a lookout for refugees from Halberstadt. Many did pass by in the course of the afternoon. They, however, knew nothing about 14 Lindenweg. They said: It's all been destroyed. Conjecture, said the colonel. He had a detailed town plan on a scale of 1:200,000 in front of him, concentrated now on the questioning of refugees, repeat-edly sent his telephone informants outside with precise questions: number of high-explosive bombs, size of the craters, which allowed conclusions to be drawn about the kind of bombs used, directions in which the fire spread, etc. That was instructive for the telephonists of the exchanges in Magdeburg, Oschersleben, Genthin listening in. It was meanwhile clear to many exchanges that this was no longer a matter of an urgent 'flash' call nor of a 'command order' but of the private search of a colonel for a best friend or a relative. Perhaps some love affair was behind his efforts?

In the course of the evening the colonel made calls in five networks, some of which extended deep into secret military spheres, if he had to pay for it all, he would soon have been poor. At about 10 p.m. a smart female telephonist in the Quedlinburg exchange hit on the idea of resorting to the SS internal connec-tion Berlin/Munich/ Halle/Weimar/Buchenwald from where Langenstein labour camp, telephone at Landhaus/Zwieberge, could be reached. By way of this complicated telephone com-munication Kuhlake got guards from the camp to look in the caves south of Halberstadt for two sisters, the owners of plot and building at 14 Lindenweg. There was presumably no one there with the names that had been passed down. Often there came the answer: They're all dead. Pure conjecture, said the colonel.

Don't talk rubbish, said the colonel agitatedly. He had the town plan in front of him. On the basis of increasingly complete entries it seemed to him quite unlikely that the fire would have taken hold of the Lindenweg part. But whether the high-explosive bombs with heavy steel casings dropped there had pen-etrated the cellars was debatable. Either because he wished for it so much or because he had learnt to make himself hard as a machine in the face of the unreliable rumour-mongering at the front, as a savvy general-staff officer, therefore, who only believed the map, he had been seized by the idea that he only had to keep on looking to discover by telephone a trace of life at 14 Lindenweg. As it later turned out his map didn't deceive him in one respect: the fire did not take hold of the houses in the area of 14 Lindenweg, because there a mass of craters, presumably the result of bombs dropped in error, had produced a kind of turned-over stony field that did not appear attractive to the flames.

Additional remark: At around lunchtime the following day one of the committed telephonists, in whom the novel, the search, of the previous day was still at work, made a call to Armed Forces High Command (improper, since she was only permitted to take requests for telephone connections but not to make connections on her own initiative nor to carry on research) with the information, that one telephone line, which did not go via the destroyed exchange at the main post office but the Regional Air Command in Dessau, led to the defence headquarters of Halberstadt in the Town Hall cellar. The result of the telephonic contact measurement was that the line was in working order right up to the receiver. But no one was answering. Thank you kindly, said the colonel. Keep on trying.

Neither person could see in their mind's eye, that the technically intact apparatus, not directly affected by the partial destruction of this cellar at 11.38 a.m. on 8 April, was lying under a 40-foot-high pile of rubble, which radiated considerable heat. Intact technology with a scrap value was buried under it. Within a radius of many hundreds of yards no living thing that could speak, neither mice nor rats. Only the technology, here: heaped-up telephone equipment, responded when it was contacted electrically with testing equipment from Magdeburg, Oschersleben or Quedlinburg. A treasure of sorts.

[The situation at the markets][17]

Fischmarkt: Hackerbräu Tavern devastated by explosive bombs, but isn't burning. On the marketplace itself smaller craters, paving stones in part torn up. The four-storey building on the north side with Café Westkamp hit by a high explosive bomb, heavy bomb damage between the street Hinter der Münze and Fischmarkt. The Fisch-markt exit of the Town Hall blocked by rubble; direct hits in parts of the Town Hall vaults; roofs blown off. Starting from the Büttner House, the Hackerbräu Tavern is burning on the left, the Gothic House on the right. Buildings between Martiniplan and Town Hall. From 3 p.m. *Firestorm*.

Wood market: Immediately after the attack Wood Market, Schmiede-strasse, Franziskanerstrasse while covered in debris give the appearance of being intact. Thirty minutes after the attack no. 4 (Stelz-Fuss) is burning, the Town Hall Pharmacy from the laboratory (in the rear building), as well as the upper storey of the Kommisse, the old customs house. Schmiede Gilde House, cellar occupants killed by bomb, is burning 50 minutes later. Is part of the firestorm from 3.30 p.m.

[Situation Schmiedestrasse] Still passable shortly after the attack, entries blocked by heaps of rubble, at 2 p.m. it's burning along its whole length. At 1.25 p.m. Fire Chief Tütschler is still in the

---

17 According to Werner Hartmann, 'Die Zerstörung Halberstadts am 8 April 1945' in *Veröffentlichungen des Städt. Museums Halberstadt, Nordharzer Jahrbuch II* (1967), pp. 39–54.

Köppen Department Store, is planning removal of the stocks of merchandise. Strong and growing heat from the fire at the Court Pharmacy. Direct hit on the central block of the Post Office, in particular telephone exchange, Post Office building not affected later by the fire.

At about 3 p.m. the Derenburg Fire Brigade tackles the Schmiede- strasse fire lane with eight hoses. It receives the order to put down a water lane along which inhabitants can get out of the burning town, a 'water cloud' of about 80 yards is maintained over the people on the roadway of Schmiedestrasse.

At 5 p.m. a group of 60 inhabitants in front of Köppen Department Store, who can't get any further, are kept under jets of water from 12 hoses (having been instructed to throw everything they had brought with them into the flames), reinforcement by the Dortmund Fire Service. That is, watered for about two hours, so that coats and clothing are damp. After that: facade of Köppen's Department Store having collapsed onto the road, the 60 can now climb over it.

[**Situation Cathedral Square**] Houses on the east side, nos 21–29, set alight from Burgtreppe, the fire 'creeps' along. Custodian Frischmeyer saves the Gleim House by getting three firemen to help him. But why should we have wanted to save this couple of oil paintings and wobbly tables? ask the helpers. What was important about them? Frischmeyer: The memory of Gleim.[18] The firemen don't know Halberstadt's cultural heritage, took determined action. The house at the corner of Cathedral Square/Tränketor is burning. The owner runs to fetch firemen. She promises each

18 Johann Wilhelm Ludwig Gleim (1719–1803), poet and friend and patron of poets.

helper several pounds of minced meat from Butcher Steinrück, Vogtei, so gets two firefighters. Cathedral and Liebfrauenkirche (Church of Our Lady) are hit by several high-explosive bombs, which is only noticed in the days that follow, since the buildings appear unshaken. It is the outward impression made by the relatively tall towers.

Beinert Family, Cathedral Square: The leaden plague cross from the east gable of the cathedral had crashed down and was lying by our front door. I tried to get it to safety, impossible because of its great weight. But it was valuable scrap, and in normal times there would have been some keen to fetch it down from the cathedral roof at night. I had often cast a glance at it. Now it lay there, but couldn't be budged.

[Situation Heinrich Julius Street/Lindenweg] Tram lines and street paving torn up 'in a particularly ugly way' by bombs, bent rails sticking up in the air. Walls of rubble. Mixed up with it palm trees, greenery from Scilla Witte's flower shop. Tongues of flame in the roof beams.

[Relationship of events to a piano lesson]

By Sunday, 8 April, Siegfried Pauli, a lad of 14 years, had practised page 59 of the *Sang und Klang* sheet music collection[19] so well that only towards the end of the 'Song of Falstaff', 'What joy, what joy, how desire drives me on',[20] did he hesitate or slow

---

19 *Sang und Klang im 19. und 20. Jahrhundert. Ernstes und Heiteres aus den Reich der Töne.* A popular collection of familiar songs and melodies, repeatedly reprinted.

20 Aria from the popular opera *The Merry Wives of Windsor* by Otto Nicolai (1810–49), based on scenes from Shakespeare.

down, but could run through more than ¾ of the piece with the prescribed arched hand. He now wanted to play it as soon as possible for his piano teacher, Fräulein Schulz-Schilling, and move on to the next page, 'Finger Exercise' by Clementini and Gilda's aria from 'Rigoletto'. The lesson was fixed for 3 p.m. the next day, Monday. The raid got in the way. 'A bomb came down 15 feet from our cellar,' related Pauli. This chain of events— raid, flight to the 'Long Cave', return to the destroyed town, the house in which the grand piano, on which he practised, stood in the smoking room, burnt to the ground—could have no influence on Siegfried's newly acquired dexterity or on his will to to press forward to page 60. The piano teacher, whom he had even encountered on the afternoon of the day of the raid, among inhabitants running this way and that on Wernigeröder Strasse, refused, referring to the destruction of the town, to take the Monday lesson. But with his indestructible will the boy found a villa at the end of Spiegelsbergen Weg, in which there was a piano, on which he repeatedly played the set piece until he got through the shaky passage just before the end without any noticeable hesitation. He practised this passage alone, always just the difficult bars, for two hours, until the owners of the villa wouldn't put up with it any more.

[Karl Lindau, resident at 8 Seidenbeutel, boilerman, coming from his workplace at 42 Hauptmann Loeper Strasse]

Threw himself down in the front garden of the Deaf and Dumb School, only the high stone bases of the railings remained, the ironwork donated for the war effort. Lindau would not have been lacking in courage, had he been able to reply with the work of his hands to the bombs being dropped on him, which ploughed over streets and gardens. He could as little reply to them, however, as to a 'locomotive or machine that had gone mad'. So he pressed himself down into the grassy soil.

Later he found his way to the cellar of the Deaf and Dumb School. He wanted to make himself useful, saw to the boiler— if need be one would have to extinguish the fire with a few large pails of water or with sand or pour water over the boiler pipes leading out of the cellar.

But with screwdriver and hammer, now at least he had something in his hands, he could do nothing against the aircraft above, which were approaching once again, just as with these tools he could not 'open' the ears and mouths of the gesticulating deaf-mutes. Here there existed a terrible limit to his labour power. In the months beforehand Lindau had repeatedly been deployed along with a bomb-disposal unit. He never expressed any fears to colleagues, but trusted in his calm and his skill. In the present situation, which had now already lasted 20 minutes, he too would have been afraid, if round him had been 16 well-built colleagues of the same sort as himself and experienced in all spheres of work, instead of the helpless deaf, frightened by the quaking of the ground, which they could feel. *It was no work detail.*

[Hurried transfer of the wounded of the Reserve Military Hospital, highest level of improvisation]

By climbing over expanses of rubble, always in the middle between burning houses, von Schroers, now saturated with news, reaches Lindenweg at the level of Roonstrasse. Here he is first of all at a loss, there can be no end to the chain of events, since the sirens for the all-clear have been destroyed (only much later does he come across a Party vehicle, on which a siren, hand-operated by a crank, is mounted). He can neither go back into

Heinrich Julius Strasse nor along Lindenweg or Roonstrasse, since the fires firmly limit what he can do. He, therefore, crosses the graveyard, the old Jewish cemetery, already thoroughly dug up once before, when Fire Pond 4 was excavated, now turned upside down once again with fancy bits of rubble. He doesn't want to walk here, not because of the fences, the completely uneven surface, but because he expects unexploded bombs or bombs with time fuses. The fire pond, evidently hit, has drained away; von Schroers is wading through the mud of the graves, does not have firm ground under his feet until he reaches the level of the pile of ruins of the Capitol Cinema.

The roof and the third floor of the family home, Hohenzollernstrasse, are burning. In principle water would be available in the pond in Bismarckstrasse, but there are no pumps. He drags furniture, bedding, instruments out of his father's surgery rooms onto the street, writes a note on a large piece of paper that he attaches to the goods.

There is absolutely no doubt that he must report to the Quedlinburg military hospital (i.e. accommodated in Halberstadt). The south side of the hospital is defended against the fires by several sets of fire-fighting appliances. Staff Doctor Ehrenbruch and von Schroers have those wounded who have been rescued loaded into military ambulances. The vehicles take them to the Klus Hills, stop in front of the entrances to the caves in which wings for aircraft are produced. In some corners fitters are still working at machine tools.

Where shall we put the wounded, sir? asks the transport officer. Tool containers were one possibility, rather cold beds, they were also reminiscent of coffins. Consequently von Schroers prefers to solve the storage problem by putting eight wounded at a time on the JU-52 transport-plane wings standing in long rows in the caves. There the wounded can talk to one another, warm one another, if they move closer together, can easily be counted. Unsolved is the question of blankets or mattresses.

Von Schroers must now urgently get to the Elysium. It's not at all clear whether the prisoners there for whose medical care he is responsible have survived. In an ambulance and making a lengthy detour by way of Langenstein and the Mahndorf estate von Schroers reaches the Elysium, a former restaurant and music hall. Twelve seriously wounded, two dead, the remainder are gathered round two cauldrons. He instructs the nurses to give injections to the seriously wounded, so that they are quiet for a while. It's all too much even for von Schroers, always keen on new experiences, he wants to temporally stretch the chain of events.

[Efforts of the head of the Red Cross, simultaneously head of the NSV (National Socialist People's Welfare Organization)]

He managed to make his way from Hardenbergstrasse to the defence HQ in Hephata Home. Here come the civilian rescuers, said Colonel Wurtinger. Detering didn't even glance at him. It was about 1 p.m., he was one and half hours late. So where are your vehicles and people? They had not escaped the massacre; that's where he was coming from. He had left his apartment on Kühlingerstrasse during the raid and immediately rushed to 18–20 Hardenbergstrasse (that was not acknowledged here). He himself had only survived because 60 feet from his goal he lay on his stomach, asphalt under him, drain beside him, could see right in front of him the direct hits on the Red Cross Emergency Centre.

With the exception of one vehicle, which at the time of the air-raid warning was on its way out to the Huy Hills on a call, no vehicles or people saved, he said. And where is the one vehicle? He was unable to specify a location. He only hoped that the voluntary helpers would go into action wherever they happened to find themselves at the time of the catastrophe. He asked for messengers, e.g. young members of the Hitler Youth on bikes or on foot in order to centralize these activities after the event at least for report purposes. He's turned down. You're mad, says the mayor.

He removed himself from this 'den of mutual destruction' where, more or less explicitly, a search for guilty parties was being conducted. But at Rescue Centre I, Plantage Park, he was also superfluous. The seriously injured, on stretchers or in blankets, waited in a large group outside. The doctors on duty and the first-aid men made their boss unwelcome. On a Red Cross bike he cycled to Wegeleben, where he was able to get a phone connection to Quedlinburg and gave the 'only sensible order that day': Send all your ambulances and helpers and doctors you can get hold of by way of Highway 12. I will be waiting for the convoy at Wegeleben turn-off. At 6 p.m. the convoy drove through the village. That same evening he flooded Hephata Home and Rescue Centres I–IV with this abundance of personnel for whom there was no room at any centre. Eighty-seven voluntary helpers came from Mahndorf in 12 vehicles, brought buttered bread, large kettles with already prepared coffee. From Rescue Centre IV, Gröperstrasse, he ordered this baggage train to the entry points of the town. Surrounded by visible success his dismissal for incompetence, issued in the course of the afternoon, reaches him at one in the morning. Out of sheer goodwill he had made a crucial mistake: instead of bringing up assistance, he would have had to stay in the Hephata Home, where, in the hours of his absence, blame was loaded onto individual shoulders.

[The deployment of the fire brigades]

As a full-time fire-service officer I was transferred here from Cologne. I am in command of the Halberstadt Service, the voluntary brigades from Derenburg and Wegeleben as well as well as parts of the full-time brigades from Hanau/Main and Dortmund caught up in the withdrawal from the west. It's all subject to the chain of command from Hephata Home, Wasserturmstrasse, and was ordered into action by me from 1 p.m.; these forces first assemble and then drive out of town when the final warning sounds. It is right first of all to hold back the forces as a whole at the exits of the town and *not* deploy them until reasonably accurate information about the *what, how, where* and the *direction* of the fires is received.

But try to adhere to this method of proceeding in the face of a nervous mayor, the town legal officer, the representatives of the Party, etc. Consequently an attack on the fire surface has to take place instantly, i.e. much too soon and quite contrary to the basic principles of a knockout blow.

You see, if from the beginning I had been able to set priorities quite unsentimentally and professionally, then in my view the Derenburg attack on Schmiedestrasse would have been pushed forward as far as Martiniplan or Holzmarkt. That would have been really interesting, because in its penny-packet form the attack soon got stuck. But pursued in a focussed form, perhaps no earlier than 3 p.m., or let's say 2.30 p.m., with all forces, except perhaps those at the *Kulk* or at *Mooshake*: then perhaps we could have split up the fire. You always have to judge the stack effect. When the pillar of hot air and debris rises to a height of several miles, then close to ground level it sucks in cold air and there you have the chimney effect, which I now have to attack. That's *always* pointless.

Water availability: Holtemme, Kulkgraben, Torteich (pond), pool of the indoor baths, fire ponds. The whole of the successful Kulk Square group drove to the indoor baths for an hour that night, where the water in the pool was still knee-high. The men splashed around in the dirty stuff for a while and could then be deployed again because they had *enjoyed* something.

The spirits factory was defended because, looking ahead, I needed to provide drinks for the men. Quite another matter were the grain silos, which had spread the fire on one flank in the direction of Salvator Hospital. We only needed a bit of an east wind and there would have been a catastrophe.

Naturally I could have saved the theatre. A group of fire-fighting vehicles to the theatre, in particular to the rear part, which is threatened from the Breiter Tor, where the combustible cult objects, shields, dragons, wooden armour, cardboard copies of houses, etc., were stored. That was a straightforward decision: have to let it burn. I could not divide up my men even more, for the simple reason that small fire-brigade groups cannot hold their position anywhere. They have to see the work the others are doing, have the impression, that as a larger group they can get out, before they commit themselves at all to attacking the fire.

You probably don't understand it from the professional point of view. In purely professional terms we had, of course, developed thanks to the extensive fires in Hamburg, Darmstadt, Cologne, that's discussed at training courses. I can completely blow out the fire for you again. Provided that I start the attack with really convincing forces, i.e. full-time fire services of six to eight big cities exactly at the right moment, shortly before the firestorm gets going.

In practical terms, however, there is nothing we can do in this 'one happy' phase. Either the brigades are not at the positions to which they have been ordered, have in part lost their way or have been prematurely directed into hopeless firetraps, etc. We are physicists, but are not allowed to do our work. We have to know about dealing with ruins, classification of exploded bombs and their results, direction of fall of incendiary devices, wind direction, direction in which building facades fall, countless individual pieces of information on the combustibility of house furnishings in order to be able to expand our professional knowledge. That would certainly be the case after the sixteenth fire disaster in a town, assuming that population and administration learn from it all.

You must not imagine that the town plan is of much help here. Instead: combustibility register of the built and rebuilt space, layout sketches of firewalls, estimates of the age of the stone used. That is no longer learnt in this war.

How do I know about the theatre? I walked through it, looked at the props and costumes department, lit up the empty stalls with my powerful pocket torches. I was also on the first floor of the old customs house and saw the town archive. So in the towns I am more or less the last person to see the valuables the town possesses, take leave, sometimes also calculate estimated values. Otherwise there's no one who bothers about such an overview of property, the inhabitants are busy with their own things. More or less on behalf of Mayor, Party, Regional Air

Command and inhabitants I take leave of the town which is essentially still standing after the attack and then let the fire take its course, because I know that the means to resist it are not organized in a focussed way.

[2 hundredweight of sausage casings]

After the last silver formation of the enemy had flown off, Tittmann, businesswoman, immediately concentrated on shifting 2 cwt of sausage casings from the store on Quedlinburger Strasse, which caught fire just after the last handcart load left, to Schützenstrasse. She had been so determined to get hold of these sausage casings, made of an intestine-like synthetic material with the description 'Special Silk Intestine' that she had bought them on Friday for Reichsmark backed up by 5 pounds of unroasted real coffee and would have been dismayed if they had burnt. Nine times she led the train of three handcarts, which had to be lifted more often than they could be pushed, along firebreaks to the backyard and cellar of Schützenstrasse 12. It was arduous, but the goods were equivalent to approximately 6,000 casings round genuine sausage meat, for which she could get at least 200 sausages in exchange, which she could exchange in turn for other goods. She secured the boxes, which gave off a strong smell, with five padlocks and an Alsatian that guarded the cellar during the night. These were black-market goods and would in a few weeks be turned into other black-market goods, which would then be much easier to store.

[The sun 'weighs' on the town, since there is hardly any shade]

After a few days beaten tracks, which more or less follow earlier routes, lead across the rubble-heaped plots and streets obscured by the world of ruins. The silence that lies over the stony devastation of the place is conspicuous. The uneventfulness is deceptive, to the extent that fires are still alive in the cellars, tenaciously making their way underground from coal cellar to coal cellar. Many scuttling small creatures. Some zones of the town stink. Corpse search parties are busy. A powerful 'silent' smell of burning lies over the town and after a few days it's experienced as familiar.

'We see how the history of industry and its objective existence, are the open book of man's essential powers, human psychology made present and perceptible . . .'

Karl Marx, 'Ökonomisch-Philosophische Manuskripte', *Marx-Engels Werke,* VOL. 40 (Berlin, 1968), p. 542 (emphases added).

Visitor From Another Star

At the end of May a visitor, James N. Eastman, Jr., came to Halberstadt, on behalf of the group of staff officers who later set up the Albert F. Simpson Historical Research Center, Maxwell Air Force Base, Alabama. He went to all the towns and cities, which 'had experienced bombing', in order to gather material for a basic psychological study. The liaison officer to the mayor's office introduced him to the civilian administration departments, he bought food packets with him 'to loosen tongues'.

That was hardly necessary, however. The people all pretty much liked to talk. But he knew almost everything in advance. He had got to know the expression: 'On that terrible day on which our beautiful city was razed to the ground', etc. The speculations as to the *meaning*, the 'stereotyped accounts of people's experiences'. He had already heard these almost factory-manufactured phrases, which fed out of mouths, in Fürth, Darmstadt, Nürnberg, Würzburg, Frankfurt, Wuppertal, etc. Did they talk in order to receive food packets? He was given quarters in a villa on Spiegelsbergen Weg within the closed area for military personnel.

Oh, you were one of those up there on 8 April? How did it look from there?

He had expected to encounter feelings of hate, some kind of reaction that put him in the ranks of the enemy. The inhabitants he questioned did not display hostility to him or to the attack.

They had settled down in the wretched, dusty area, on the fringes of the destruction, by which they settled as by a dried-up lake.

But an air of sadness hung over the whole thing. To the question: Would you like to emigrate to the United States, 82 per cent answered: Very much! When will that be possible? You're kidding. It's not possible at all. It was clear: if everything was changing anyway, they wanted to continue the change as fast as possible, they wanted to get away.

Even where materials were obviously available there were no discernible attempts at reconstruction. A total of six attempts in the town to erect a roof for a ground floor on damaged foundation walls. All these cases upper middle class. In lower middle class and lower class no examples of a will to build . . .

The starting point of his study was the assumption that these unnecessary bombing raids created tenacious enemies, who would not stop thinking of revenge. A new edition, therefore, of the 'Versailles' way of thinking which the postwar policies of the Allies would have to reckon with. The hypothesis could not be confirmed. Would he like another piece of cake? The woman whom he was asking questions had cake from Emersleben.[21]

The question, whether those affected would be willing to go through with it all again was a naive one; it was worked into the questionnaire as index for the *lie scale*. Would those questioned prefer to commit suicide? One never knows whether one's going to get it. Suicide would probably always be too soon. What would be the next most serious thing they would undertake to avoid an air raid?—There will probably be no more air raids now. The situation was a 100 years back.

21 Then, however, he did know how he could measure a deeper activity. He only had to lay out things of value, e.g. presents, in the manner of a mousetrap, go out (he could secure them in some way, so that an effort had to be made to get them. So something worth stealing 'openly hidden' or left lying in front of the person questioned. Hence he could determine 'depth activity' in the shape of the 'take-away energy' (how quickly it was stolen). He called it 'production energy', dependent on the capacity 'to produce needs, so basically—need energy'. In this respect, there were significant differences on his scale. In the case of those *extremely affected* or *not at all affected* by the raid, there was relatively little energy in the sense of wanting to have. In the case of all intermediate values: high-energy yields, going as far as attempts at open robbery, wrestling with the questioner, e.g. over a box of tobacco. Effectively, everyone stole, but the measurement of the time taken, of the inventive inputs, in particular the measurement of the threshold to be overcome, *extremely variable*.

From the town archivist he requested a list of all fires in the town since 1123. On the list 8 April 1945 had been 'forgotten'. Named were 44 large conflagrations, the majority of them in the Middle Ages. The man lamented each of these historical fires, and, in particular, art treasures destroyed in churches.

Another method: Free reporting of what those interviewed had done on the day of the raid. Usually after a few phrases devoid of perception there came an exact description of the escape from the town. Or that on 11 April, 'the day your tanks occupied the town', aircraft had flown very low over the expanse of ruins, 'inspecting' it.[22]

It was impossible to distinguish whether they wanted revenge. Aside from a deep stratum, which perhaps he did not reach (somehow the lie scale didn't work), they were as barren and empty as the surface of the town on which the sun beat down. Had we bombed them into being friends of our nation?

It seemed to him as if the population, despite an inborn pleasure in telling stories had, precisely within the contours of the destroyed areas of the town, lost the psychic strength to remember.[23]

22 Statement of a grammar-school teacher, at present detailed to burying the dead; subjects: Latin, physics, biology; Party member (hence now burial squad): 'Two young women, pregnant, resident in Krebsschere Lane, fleeing together. Loss of consciousness. Premature birth as bodies burn. The new life likewise burns [. . .] Respectfully, we allow this horror to remain lying on the street for one more day.'

23 Key heading: 'Now we don't need to worry any more, because we don't have anything.' How was poor Eastman supposed to note down the tone colour of this sentence? He too had only his impression to go by, could not break down the qualitative remark into overtones, proportions of exultation, melancholy, etc. But he had the impression that for the person interviewed, as for many others before her, 'home town', family and other dead, a family property, a neighbourhood burnt down, etc., had not only been positively connoted but were also linked to feelings of protest. So that on the one hand she was moved by sadness yet on the other

Qualitative answer of an interviewee: 'Having come to a particular point of horror, it no longer matters who was responsible for it: one just wants it to end.'

was quite pleased at the 'change that had taken place'. On no account did Eastman want to appear cynical. To that extent, he felt himself quite inhibited at evaluating the statements.

What Does 'Really' Mean in Retrospect?

17 MORE STORIES ABOUT THE AIR WAR

Dragonflies of Death

In the blue sky we sense
Assyrian dragonfly wings
And the lowest layer of the obscured sky
Is darkened by the storm of war

Osip Mandelstam

The Russian poet sat in his usual place in a Moscow cafe. The ventilator hummed. Scraps of hit songs. Outside a bright spring day. No word of darkening, as the world had darkened on the death of the Son of God. A considerable interval of time still to come before war will descend on this land. And even then the war did not seize hold of the plot on which the cafe was situated, in which the man, who was writing and who, one way or another, will have been killed in a few years, sat in temporary safety.

None of the Soviet publishers on whose payments the poet lived thought much of what he produced. He did not provide, they asserted, any useful texts. They employed him to make translations from European languages; they themselves didn't dare let this man, of whom other poets said he possessed special qualities, starve or destroy him. They were superstitious. They were not so firmly convinced of their own necessity, that they denied the right to existence of an (obstinate) fellow citizen. The poet's hands touched the cold marble surface of the cafe table. While he was writing, no storm of war. 'The Assyrian prisoners crawl like chicks under the feet of the giant Emperor.' But in the cafe there were no Assyrian prisoners and also no Emperor. There was building work going on at the entrance hall of the underground station on the square opposite the cafe.

The words flew across the paper. This poet radiated stubborn consciousness.

Natalya Goncharova, *Angels and airplanes.*
'In the blue sky we sense / Assyrian dragonfly wings.'

On that day, far from the poet's seat in Moscow, Italian pilots, in aircraft whose cells the engineers had skilfully structured like insect bodies, and whose fuselages were painted, dropped bombs, each one custom-made, on targets in the karst mountains of Abyssinia which possessed of human souls, could find no escape on any side. They were killed by high-explosive or rock splinters. That was what the poet was writing about. He had seen nothing of it.

Nor was he able to observe a column of Chinese infantry who, even before the end of that day marched into a trap.

—Is the angel Asrail in the poem an allusion to Stalin?

—You mean Stalin is 'the strong hand who raises his sceptre in the world'? I don't think so. The poet isn't making any definite allusions.

—But he expresses a wish that something be 'swept away by force'?

—Not by Stalin.

—The poet fears a danger that is not specific. He would like to see it replaced by a specific one. That could also be Stalin and his persecuting authorities.

—I don't believe the poet considered Stalin to be so powerful. 'Stalin is unable to place a conquered sky under his high protection.'

And laboriously making progress
in the scales of maimed wings
Asrail takes the conquered sky
under his high protection.

Commentary on 'Dragonflies of Death'

'*Assyrian*': 'There are epochs that say individual men are of no concern to them, that one must use them like bricks, that one must build from them and not for them. The Assyrian master builders treat the human mass like material of which there must be enough and which must be delivered in large quantities' (Ossip Mandelstam, 'Humanism and the Present', 1923).

'*Dragonfly wings*': Insect species with a long body and membranous wings. Is counted among the great predators, the outstanding fliers. The colours and segmentation characteristic of dragonflies served as models for the warplanes of the early 1920s which were not yet produced industrially but in craft-manufacturing processes. They are used for offensive military purposes in Spanish Morocco, Libya, China but, after 1918, no longer on the European continent. A Russian witness cannot have seen them.

'*The lowest layer of the obscured sky*': According to Thomas Aquinas, this layer lies inside us. It cannot be perceived through observation from outside.

'*storm of war*': Clichéd phrase or comparison, as wars do not have the structure of thunderstorms. Lightning, downpours, thick cloud, thunder are the least important characteristics of destructive effects in war.

'*Asrail*': Exterminating Angel or Angel of Death. Seizes power over the 'conquered skies' as soon as these have been abandoned by 'all good spirits'. Something that darkens the heart of the poet becomes aware of this giant being and even wishes that Asrail assumes power. The threatening danger thereby becomes something definite. It draws together in the heart of the poet the misfortunes scattered across the earth and shuts them up there. To that extent, the poet and Asrail are companions.

The Dragonfly

In a basin of the Alps, which in the Grisons rise to a height of more than 13,000 feet, there lies a green-coloured lake with untouched plant life in its depths. This place is virtually unchanged since the upfolding of the mountains, i.e. for 200,000 years, says the geologist Schweickart.

On this sunny day dragonflies were flying round the surface of the water. Impossible for them ever to fly over the surrounding mountain ridges. Measured in human steps, it was a day's journey to the next body of water.

Hence a special kind of dragonfly had developed here, with a dark brown growth of little hairs between the seventh and eighth segments. Unmistakeable feature of the dragonfly group in this location. They would have torn any intruding dragonfly to pieces.

My father caught one of these 200,000-year-old aristocrats in 1938 and released it on the pond of his garden. It lived there, exiled from home, for another seven years and perished when the garden burnt in the firestorm. The pond, a concrete construction, burst, and when the fire broke out no water remained in it.

In winter, which is severe at 13,000 feet, the dragonflies lodge themselves in tiny irregularities, which their element, water, provides on the edges of the ice.

The Long Paths to Knowledge

At first, the inhabitants of Halberstadt believed that the destruction was a temporary state of affairs. The town would be rebuilt just as it had been before. They believed that until the autumn of 1945.

On Bismarckstrasse a house had burnt right down to the first floor. Already in June 1945, work began on covering the stone structure which was open to the sky with roofing paper. So the ground floor and the cellar were protected from autumn rain and winter storms.

Then many inhabitants moved away. On the edges of the town, crowds of refugees settled into the estates that had not been touched by the bombs. They came in seven batches. In the middle of the town there remained the crater.

The municipal administration maintained the 'idea of the town' as 'organizational skeleton' for another 50 years. Later, ministers' sons set themselves at the head of the movement to save mediaeval buildings and to reform the administration. It was their aim to build a meeting place on the site of St Martin's Church, i.e. of the church interior, which had once belonged to the town council, as a starting point from which the crater left by the war could be resettled. This is evidently the terrain on which a new town can successfully be built.

Gradually it reaches even people's hearts, that the damage of 8 April 1945, done in 20 minutes, is a conclusive fact.

What Does 'Really' Mean in Retrospect?

Over the spot on which our house had stood (after the destruction it still stood for a while as a ruin facing in the same direction as always) blocks of flats were put up at right angles to it. The blocks are in a row with one sidewall to the street. The earlier townspeople's houses, on the other hand, provided depth, from the street away to the garden at the back. These ground plans have been obliterated. The swifts, whose cries dominate the evening, belong to the same tribe as those of 1936. They did not return from their long-distance flights until after the disaster, but re-established themselves in the stony desert, geographically at the same places, within feet of where they had been before.

Where the garden was there is now a space for recreational sport. A group of bushes with white inedible berries has survived, they've asserted themselves against the new gardening approach of the estate. Apart from that there's a stone that was brought here from the Huy Ridge. It had a purpose in the rock garden, but is now without purpose.

What is real about this arrangement of remains? Six bushes and a stone cannot produce any kind of reality. But something earlier, that lives in my mind, and the seven particles form an ELEMENT. Reality emerges from such elements.

On this day, the day of remembrance of the air raid of 8 April 1945, we learn that the three formations which ploughed up the centre of the town and set it alight had not flown from the direction of Magdeburg, from east to west as we had assumed at the time, going by our hearing, our imagination, the apparent direction of the detonations. They came from the south, from the Harz Mountains. They were following a plan, which was almost not carried out, since two other targets of equal standing were competing with our town in the 'target reserve'. A miscalculation and an error led to the plan being executed. Now, 60 years later, we learnt how little necessity there was to this event. In accordance with the plan a prominent building, the girls' grammar school erected in 1912, with its three wings (and a red reflecting roof) was the so-called point zero of the attack. Such a point zero is a safe place, because it first of all has to be flown over, before, after a fixed number of seconds, the bombardiers release the bomb load. From the familiar 'point zero of the attack' (we, however, had never seen the building, an educational establishment designed with reforming views in mind, as the starting point of a deadly attack), the aircraft of the middle bomber group covered the distance that brought them to 50 yards from the cellar in which we were sheltering, in six seconds. The bombs fall at an angle, they reach the ground forward of the point from which they have been dropped. We should, in fact, have been hit; the movement of the air above the town makes for a difference of 2 to 7 yards. To that extent, it was not 'real' (i.e. not out of a logic of causality, derived from the context, entrusted only to the chance winds), that we survived. Twenty minutes later, feeling nothing but panic, i.e. alive, we hurried towards the edge of town.

Love 1944

The uncertainty, above all the lack of influence on whether and when someone will be struck down by the war, makes the soul bold.

So, after an air raid on Ulm, which went on for hours, Gerda F. did not save herself up any longer. No thought of waiting for one of the returning warriors, whom she still knew and who would ask for her hand. She didn't want to get to know any better those left behind in the armaments factories of the place. All were looking for closeness. She took a man who was passing through town up to her room. They never saw each other again. There was nothing about it that she regretted.

> For one night full of bliss
> I would give my all.[1]

Cooperative Behaviour

After the air raid of 11 February 1943 the charred remains of a man were found in a house in Blaubach. One resident of the house maintained, that they were the remains of her husband. A second woman from the same house declared, her husband had likewise been sitting in this destroyed cellar, probably one was sitting next to the other. These were also the remains of her husband's body. She too would want to be able to visit a grave. At that the woman who had first returned to the ruined building[2] suggested dividing the remains of the charred man.

---

1 'Für eine Nacht voller Seligkeit / Da geb ich alles hin'—lines from a 1940s' hit, sung by Marika Rökk in the film *Kora Terry*. [Trans.]

2 When the girl, Franziska Ziegler, who had gone to a public shelter at the beginning of the raid, returned, only the left firewall of her house was still standing. She was joined by her 18-year-old sister. Martha and Viktor Ziegler were standing upright against the wall with rubble up to their chests. When the girls called out to their father, his head fell forward. The ceiling of the cellar, a concrete rectangle, was hanging by a single iron loop. They fetched petrol and tried to burn the dead. 'If we don't do it, they'll be eaten by the rats.' They had to do it.

Fires inside People

Detectives in heavy protective clothing are examining the dead. They are recruited not because any features of the crime are puzzling, but because the individual assignment of the dead to name, place of residence, close relatives, workplace—that is, individualization—demands criminological experience. What could criminal prosecution achieve at a moment when what is needed is something like the restoration of a RELATIONSHIP TO REALITY? Anonymous dead, people roaming around trying to find answers, looking for their nearest and dearest, destroy the idea of reality more effectively than an air raid, which, after all, adds something very *real* to all reality.

—You use the words normality and reality as if they meant the same thing?

—It's impossible to talk about normality.

—And what do you mean by *reality*?

—A state of affairs, in which Party and state still appear to be doing something. Hence the cauldrons of barley soup with a large proportion of meat—cooked in advance and driven from country estates into the town—are a contribution to restoring a relationship to reality at certain road junctions.

The fire-brigade lieutenant was talking to a member of a study group from the Reich Propaganda Ministry which was looking at the problem sociologically ('population studies'): What actually happens in people's heads when their town is destroyed? They are neither disheartened nor is their morale so affected that they want a peace agreement nor are they prompted to rebel against the authorities. All that results is a CONFUSION OF SENSE. It may be that they are uncertain whether what they are experiencing is reality or dream. How should the political leadership respond to this intermediate state of mind?

On the other hand, states the report of a parallel study group of Section II of Reich Security Head Office (RSHA), a fantastic alteration of all mental states, prompted by the fire storm, razing of the town, and loss of contacts with reality, could PROVOKE A RUPTURE WITH BOURGEOIS EXIS-TENCE, releasing reserves of strength for the FINAL BATTLE. What do we know, said SS Colonel Eberlein to fire-brigade officer Künnecke, about what powers are still present in desperate people, before which the enemy should have a HOLY DREAD. Because it is not only bombs that explode or cities that burn, but inside men there are bombs that burn up reality. How, responded Künnecke, do you intend to direct this inner fire against a PARTICULAR ENEMY? To the best of my knowledge fire moves outwards in all directions simultaneously, in rings.

They were drinking Nordhäuser schnapps. A comforting atmosphere arose, so that they felt united in their feeling of help-lessness. When it came to the FIRES IN MEN'S HEARTS, one was unable to put them out, and the other was unable to direct them.

Zoo Animals in the Air Raids

Early in the morning of the day following the night raid on Hamburg two fire-brigade sub-officers arrived at the devastated grounds of the Hagenbeck Zoo. Bleary-eyed, yet tense enough to be ready for action, at this hour the fire brigade took posses-sion of the city again.

All the animals were behaving calmly. They displayed no urge to escape. The elephants crowded close to the two matriarchs. Eagles and aviary birds had remained in their enclosures for hours even though there was no wire mesh to prevent them spreading around the grounds. Bodies of animals, craters. No nervousness among the remaining creatures, which were aware after all of the death of their companions. This was evident from the distance they kept from the carcasses. From the point of view of fire prevention there was nothing to be clarified. It had not been fire, but sheer explosive force that had shattered the equilibrium of the zoo. The animals seemed to take the intrusion as something *alien* to them. They had returned to their daily lives.

Are animals so forgetful that a few minutes or hours later they no longer remember the terrors, panic-stricken at the moment of the attack, afterwards so impassive? The two officers appeared shaken, not by the consequences of the raid, but by the silence which lay over the remaining stock of the zoo and which feigned a kind of PATIENCE OF NATURE in which they were unable to believe.

What could be stated about that in their report? It was not the time for theoretical reflections. Back at the improvised headquarters at the edge of the city the two sub-officers were assigned to further reconnaissance expeditions.[3]

---

3 The headquarters of the Hamburg Fire Brigade had itself fallen victim to the flames. On the street leading to the headquarters, burnt-out fire engines could be seen under the rubble. They had tried to get through to the building to save it. Overtaken by the firestorm, they burnt and then were buried by collapsing facades.

What Holds Voluntary Actions Together?

'And if you do not commit your life, you will never win life . . .' At the risk of her life Sigrid Berger has rescued a little dog at the corner of Gneisenaustrasse. Why, asks Frau Schaffner, did you risk your life? Frau Berger did it 'without thinking'. Something living whimpered. At that she lost her head.

In May 1944, Fireman Büttner has been ordered with his fire engine to tackle an emergency at an industrial plant struck by bombs. On his way to the scene of the blaze, he drives past his own house, sees that it has been destroyed. He does not know if his family has been saved. But he is part of a convoy of 29 fire engines, the vehicles more or less push Büttner along the chain of command to his place of deployment.

In the plant that has been attacked chemical stores have been hit; the bombs find allies on the ground, as it were. There is nothing that can be extinguished or cleared. Büttner has put on his gas mask, which, he says, is no use in a real emergency. This is the emergency, replies Mückert. Büttner hesitated to agree, since he does not yet know whether his family has been saved.

RIGHT: In a single night's duty as a fire-fighter (fire-fighting was pointless, however) in Wuppertal, Gerlach saves 17 people.

ABOVE: Fred Gerlach.

A certain degree of forgetfulness of self is required, says Gerlach. Necessity alone, the prospect of a medal was not sufficient, at the moment of danger, for one to run into a burning house. It's more the thought: 'I'll find someone in there, save her, and at a glittering ball she'll make me happy.' So I follow the child who led me into the house, which is close to collapse. The fire had taken hold of the second floor. I found a woman lying there, unconscious, whom I could not carry down the stairs alone. So I first of all saved the child, who was leading me, and whose mother the woman, lying in the smoke of the first floor, appeared to be. I was really unhappy that I was unable to help this woman. The child pressed against me, pulled me towards the collapsing building. A female first-aid attendant came past. With her help I brought the unconscious woman, who had smoke poisoning, from the first floor down to the street, where the child kept watch over her. I thought I discerned a certain acknowledgment in the eyes of the young first-aid attendant . . .

Graduate engineer Lukomski, Polish Reserve Officer, grabs the phosphorus bomb and puts it in a pail of water. The German factory was a matter of complete indifference to him.

Lukomski answering the telephone call of the Gauleiter, who congratulates him on his action and promises a special allocation of rations. Lukomski thanks the Gauleiter. He cannot reply that he had *not* done it for a reward; he had done it 'without wanting to'. It's normal, that's why we did it. It had already been **practised** like that in Poland. Now what has been **practised** benefits the enemy. Of course, he cannot say that to the Gauleiter.

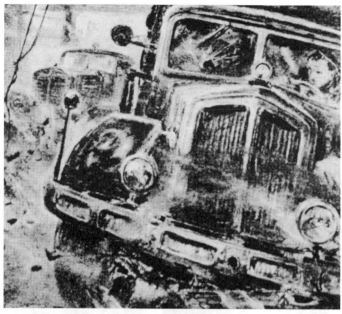

In another factory loaded Hanomag long-distance trucks are standing in a basement threatened by collapse. B. Friedrich and Gert Paasche, who became friends about 20 minutes before, turn driving the 23 heavy vehicles out of the basement through the fire and rubble, away from the factory site and out of town, into an adventure. They were curious whether they would manage it. The incident brought them closer together. 'Realistic handling of risks.'

Friends. Yesterday they didn't know each other. Meanwhile, 23 trucks have been saved.

Frau Schaffner, Frau Dänicke, Sigrid Berger, Maria Plitsche. At a party. They found one another again after the fires of the night of the air raid.

LEFT: Maria Plitsche leads into the open a group trapped in a cellar by rubble.
RIGHT: Risking her life, Frau Dänicke brings supplies out of the Provisions Store.

Frau Dänicke's fiancé. Reproached her for having taken risks and on top of that handing over the boxes of biscuits. Where could I have stored them? retorted Frau Dänicke. Six months later her fiancé was dead.

WHAT HOLDS VOLUNTARY ACTIONS TOGETHER?

Fire-Brigade Commander W. Schönecke Reports

As darkness began to fall on 12 Sept. 1944 we observed the
approach of various enemy bomber formations from our command post in a manor house east of Cologne. The fire engines
were partly drawn up under the lime trees of the village square,
partly in a little pine wood nearby. Basically we go by the Confi-
dential Air Situation Report of the Reich Rail Administration,
which provides a more accurate picture than those of the Air
Raid Warning Centres, which report for the wireless networks,
i.e. for all the civilians in the Reich. Then the Fifth RAF Bomber
Fleet over the Eifel Hills is identified as the main threat of the
night. That turned out more or less to be the fan attack on
Darmstadt between 9 and 10 p.m. Fire pre-culmination as early
as 10.20 p.m. Rescue groups from outside are engaged in pene-
trating the chaos. From a distance of more than 200 miles we
'see' that as quite pointless, we see it purely from our experience
and from the enemy's method of setting the town alight from all
sides simultaneously and narrowing the escape routes. It's an
intelligent application of the basic idea of the Battle of Cannae,[4]
i.e. with a northern arm the fire reaches round the town, while
the southern arm closes off the opposite side with fires. If I men-
tion experience here, then I mean the telephone calls with other
fire services which we immediately made, the conversations in the
command post, in other words, the shared knowledge of a large
number of professionals.

I immediately, i.e. at 9.50 p.m., had a column of fire-brigade
vehicles set out from the direction of Cologne, and at six in the
morning, practically when the fire was over, we came upon a

---

4 Cannae (216 BC): Battle in the Second Punic War in which the Carthaginian commander Hannibal destroyed a Roman army using a double-envelopment tactic.
[Trans.]

concentration of 6,200 fire-service men, professionally trained gentlemen from Würzburg, Karlsruhe, Mannheim, Frankfurt/ Main, etc., 390 vehicles altogether, on the stretch of autobahn west of Darmstadt and east of Mannheim. Still standing on the main line to Mannheim is a train which had steamed out of Darmstadt Central Station when the final warning siren sounded. On board are 1,000 men of the Organisation Todt, who had been working on the West Wall defences. This whole rescue and fire force, had it been available seven to eight hours earlier, could have broken up the area affected by the fire, always assuming it had not been a fan attack and no delayed action bombs had been dropped. In this case it was hopeless.

So we passed the morning there and at about 12 midday drove back to Cologne on the autobahn.

Much more favourable, in particular as far as the speed of our arrival at the place of the disaster is concerned, was the Wuppertal night. We called it 'a night in Venice',[5] because one would have thought water was available in sufficient quantity since the River Wupper flowed along the middle of the valley. But the firestorm swept over the water with embers and gusts of flames, so that even wooden piles and groups of piles (mooring posts) burnt down to the surface of the water. A human head ducked below the water except for the nose corresponds for example to a mooring post.

As I've already said, with respect simply to the place, water was there; the fire-brigade units coming from the west arrived in good time but we were unable to get down into the narrow valley, and were forced to look down on the turmoil from the heights on both sides. We could very well see the fire-service units ready

5 'A Night in Venice', title of a popular operetta composed by Johann Strauss. [Trans.]

and waiting on the ridge on the other side of the valley, greetings passed back and forward, radio messages. It first of all had to burn out, before we could go in, we could not, however, extend the operation that long.

Basically it was like this: the RAF drops cascades. The US Air Force carpets a target with bombs. The strategic bombing of the city centres, where some substance is still assumed, sets intersecting bomb lines which broke up the town into a number of X patterns—one might also say, like sword cuts on the bald head of a member of a duelling fraternity—and then set it alight. The time-fuse bomb, which would have stopped the fire-brigade units, corresponds to the short fuse HB 4,000-pounder with a delay of 30 to 60 minutes. But, as already mentioned, the fire-service units could in any case not get down to Wuppertal, Elberfeld, Barmen, that is the city stretching for many miles along the valley, not from one side nor the other.

Urban quadrangles, or as the layman puts it: blocks of housing, burn 6 to 9 yards a minute. The weight of bay windows and turrets, i.e. in particular, superstructures on corner buildings, represents a significant additional pressure. It has to be taken into consideration that the line of the vaulting and of the roof pressure descends close to foot of the building, at the outer wall. At these points the walls tip over.

Here the AP (armour-piercing) 13,500-pounder, 6 tonnes, is the queen of safe-cracking bombs, rocket-powered. It easily cuts through 10-foot-thick reinforced concrete ceilings. What were we supposed to do about that? From that point of view one would have had to build the cities quite differently. In particular not place them in narrow valleys. The educational system of the many laypersons who constitute the population of a town or city or of a Reich would have had to be reorganized. They wall up the cellar windows, e.g. in order to find shelter, and then can't escape. Columns of fire vehicles, which have halted in burning streets—they have goals to which they are ordered to adhere, after all, even if for they moment they are inactive—are surrounded by hysterical people who want the firemen to lay hoses from the nearest hydrant and play them on the burning buildings. By the time this mass of water gets into the cellars, however, it's boiling hot. Who can exclude the possibility that there are not still inhabitants in these cellars?

If it is true that *firefighting experience* must be a reflection of the *enemy attack*, then the training of the firefighter has to be radically changed. With our skills and numbers we didn't get anywhere near the important points. Professional firefighting is, therefore, the appropriate reorganization of the whole society, its mode of building, its people, starting with six-year-old children, whose ABC is of no use whatsoever against the bomber squadrons. It's not as if I say so out of despair; our warning, e.g. against entering the concrete bunkers in Frankfurt/Main or Mannheim, which attracted the 24,000-pound bombs or the APs and which constituted the main danger points because of the thickness of the reinforced concrete, went by radio to colleagues who knew that anyway, whereas we had hardly any possibility of getting this information to the people crowding round the bunker entrances. Rather it was the case, for example in April '45, that on the basis of our experience—which we could never have gathered in peace time—we really had the impression that we could get a grip on the thing, if we only sufficiently thoroughly clarified the conditions as given above. It's not a matter for businessmen, Party organizations, industrialists, property owners, civil servants, military men, etc., or whoever may govern such a population, but—with the view of Wuppertal from the hills in mind—of fire-fighting in all its identifiable scope.

The Run-Up to the Catastrophe

Perhaps the objects around us derive their
immobility only from our certainty that they are
what they are and not anything else; they gain their
immobility from the inflexibility of the thinking with
which we respond to them.
Robert Musil

Everyone thought he was crazy. In a section of the office on the 57th floor, where he was tolerated because he occasionally produced design ideas, he painted pictures of himself in which he was pierced through by skewers but soon also by aircraft and drag-onflies, a latter-day St Sebastian. He hardly dared tell anyone.

Then, when the catastrophe occurred, not immediately rec-ognizable as such to the occupants of the giant silo, a surprise something like a weather catastrophe, something singular, only per-ceived as an event by way of broadcasts, he was one of the first to run down the 57 storeys on foot and *saved* himself, reaching one of the first-aid posts which were situated more than 700 yards from the twin towers. Quite the opposite of his fantasies. Untouched, not even with a noticeable covering of dust, he watched the col-lapse of the towers from his rescue cave.

He could not have said that he had a presentiment of the event. His creative ideas, which, it was later maintained, displayed a prophetic gift, bore no relationship to actual circumstances. The opening of an exhibition is needed to bring them and reality together.

It was quite a different matter with Romuald Davidson, a disaster-management and fire-service expert. He had no interest whatsoever in artistic approaches. He was the author of a report, it even impressed the insurance companies which three weeks before the collapse of the towers were mulling over the conditions of the insurance cover. The report stated that a shock at any point of intersection of these steel-protected buildings, whether from outside, inside or from an earthquake, could not upset their general stability. Indeed, significant equilibriums were a given here. If the west edge of the tower is placed under excessive gravitational pressure as compared to the east edge, the north edge and the south edge of each tower balance the pull. Over 800 pages the university-trained engineer and stress analyst, accredited at three New York universities, made every effort to keep the flow of probabilities on the right side of a meaningful prediction. Nothing in the report can be called negligent.

What was unusual about the disaster of 11 September was the particular arbitrariness and, to some extent, carelessness of the attackers. They had not calculated anything exactly. Everything was more or less guesswork. It was this very imprecision that allowed them to penetrate the seam between IMPROBABLE and JUST ABOUT PROBABLE. This joint is especially hard for stress analysts to calculate.

PLANNED COUNTERMEASURES TO THE CATASTROPHE

Planned countermeasures to the catastrophe

Water for the sprinkler systems fed from the absolute ceiling of the building. These systems sprayed water with great precision on the storeys affected, also those not affected, up to the level of the penetration.

—No more than a drop of water on a hot stone?

—In the event of danger on this scale a sprinkler sprays quite a lot of water. I wouldn't call it a drop.

—Ineffective nevertheless?

—On those floors on which kerosene wasn't burning, a very successful safety measure. Futile, of course, where the fire was raging.

Helicopter landing pads on the flat roof of the skyscrapers.

—Would it have been feasible to evacuate people from the upper storeys?

—One could see the people at the windows of the upper floors.

—Could they have been brought up to the helicopters by ropes?

THAT WAS PRACTISED. THE EVACUATION OF MORE THAN 3,000 PEOPLE, ATTEMPTING TO SAVE THEMSELVES ON THE ROOF OF ONE OF THE TOWERS, WOULD HAVE BEEN POSSIBLE WITH SPECIALIST UNITS WITH HELICOPTERS, ASSUMING ANY LANDING WOULD NOT HAVE BEEN MADE IMPOSSIBLE BY MOVEMENT OF THE BUILDING AND HIGH SMOKE LEVELS. The helicopter pilots, however, who approached the buildings were not professionally trained. They would have been able to clarify traffic accidents, communicate news about New York City. Helicopter pilots with the requisite training only arrived after the collapse of the buildings.

Iron construction and fire service

—How many engineers are there in the New York Fire Department who are experts in iron construction?

—Eighty-seven.

—Were they on the spot?

—They had to be called together. Twelve were on holiday, 16 had been seconded to the missile-shield project, which requires specialist expert knowledge. They were writing a report.

—What was the advice of the three who arrived in time?

—There is hardly any experience of conditions on this scale. They said it was possible to count on a degree of tenacity of the steel construction. Who would ever have made calculations in anticipation of such an occurrence?

In wartime, there are air-raid shelters, bunkers, it was said in the subsequent debate. For the occupants of the sky-scraper towers who were crushed in the collapse as in a mill there were no containers to which they could flee, no rescue zones.

—Viennese fire-service experts, with experience of rescue operations in Alpine tunnels and with accidents affecting cable cars, maintained a chance to rescue those trapped in caverns had been missed.

—You mean the intense communication between mobile phones in the ruins and offices outside which continued for one and a half days?

—Exactly. As in giant ocean-going liners which sink to the bottom of the sea, bubbles form thanks to steel girders and cavities in the silicon ruins, caves in which it is possible to breathe, perhaps only enough for two to twenty-four people. So maintained the Viennese.

—Speculation?

—We don't know. According to statistical probability such cavities must form. And where there are cavities there is the possibility of rescue.

—But what is likely in this occurrence as a whole?

—Nothing, as far as cavities are concerned. The experience comes from mining accidents.

—The rescuers from Vienna who championed this theory had got their luggage ready for a flight to New York?

—They were ready to travel.

—And why were they not called on?

—I don't think it was pride. The requests were lost in the haste and confusion. The Viennese waited, the New Yorkers didn't know, at least not in the relevant office, that the Viennese were waiting for an answer.

—The Viennese would have had to fly immediately.

—Without waiting for a reply?

—Correct.

—And who would have paid for the flight?

—In the event of success that would have been taken care of.

Inexplicable Reactions in Sandstone Rock

If Hitler stands by Volga's shore
Then the Rhine cathedrals sink down one by one.

A fortune-teller in Switzerland called Regnon C. Iturbé had made
assertions which, in August 1942, caused the regional adminis-
trators and civil-protection officials of the Rhineland serious concern. They sent their works department heads to the cathedrals.
And, in fact, a fantastic disease had taken hold of the naves along
the Rhine. The sandstone was leaking. The initial suspicion. But
what a terrible sight it would be if the mighty buildings were
reduced to a heap of sand in the middle of the cities.

Those in charge of air-raid protection and disaster manage-
ment are identical. Both are in the hands of the regional admin-
istrators. The possibility that the phenomenon had anything to
do with the night-time attacks of the Royal Air Force could be
discounted. Instead it was remarkable that explosive and incendiary bombs so rarely struck the mighty churches that provided
such big targets. No intention was supposed on the part of the
attackers. A night attack is just as little able to exactly hit a target
as the planners of the attack were in a position to completely
avoid targets.

A causal relationship between tremors as a result of the
bombing and the remarkable 'internal flow of the sands in the
masonry of churches' was also excluded, because cathedrals in
towns that had not been attacked showed the same findings as
cathedrals in towns that had been attacked.

That month the lead formations of the 24th Tank Corps
had broken through to the Volga. A summertime river of vast
breadth. Some agriculture (including greenhouses) and industry

scattered along the length of the river. The Führer had not visited this front. It could not be said that 'Hitler stands by Volga's shore'. On the other hand the disintegration of the Rhineland cathedrals was also just beginning.

Punishment of the Swiss fortuneteller or ordering him to remain silent were out of the question. The exchange of views at the level of the military authorities was made more difficult by the extreme secrecy required in the affair. How should one express oneself? How was it possible to avoid arousing suspicion that one believed the prediction, or on the other hand counter the catastrophic result if it turned out to be true? Prevent Hitler from travelling to the Volga? How was it possible to know if he was planning such a thing at all?

Erich Löwe, a senior civil servant and cheery Rhinelander came up with the only practical solution. It had already been announced that the cathedrals would be protected against bomb damage by scaffolding and by a layer of cement round the bottom of the walls. Assuming heavenly forces were not at work, that supported the buildings, even 'if their hour-glass was running out'. Ultimately, said the construction expert, the churches could be rebuilt in concrete even before they had completely disintegrated in their sandstone form.

—They would then be no more than an EXTERIOR MOULD, Party Comrade Löwe?

—Indestructible.

—The twelfth-century interior, however, would be destroyed because of the sand trickling away?

—Would have to be redone.

—There would be nothing sacred about the protective structure?

—Sacredness is not a matter of building materials.

Then in the winter, the sand in the cathedrals along the Rhine stopped running out. Had the cathedrals perhaps been at risk from dry east winds as they prevailed in July and August 1942? When the westerly air currents with their aggressive centuries-old winds returned towards the end of the year, the giant buildings settled down.

How the 'Flying Fortresses' Disappeared in Lake Constance

The 'Flying Fortresses' which headed out across Lake Constance leaving the airspace above the town of Friedrichshafen behind, had to be counted as lost. From the outside they still looked like big aircraft, but inside they were wrecked by anti-aircraft shells; some were on fire. These aircraft over the lake were out of control. Otherwise, they would have turned westwards when they were still over land and from there begun the flight home. About the middle of the lake—we were watching the calamity from the Swiss side—they tilted downwards day after day, finally striking the water. A few parachutes with dead aircrew hanging from them.

The boats of our border police marked the spots up to the point to which Swiss neutrality extended. Rescue services or police were not allowed to go any further on the lake. The bombers always came down before this line.

There was a particular pig-headedness in the way the planners of these raids on Friedrichshafen again and again launched their heavy aircraft at the industrial plants that lay to one side of the town. The factories had long ago been destroyed. They were nevertheless defended by the German anti-aircraft batteries in so-called anti-aircraft traps. Defended with the same obstinacy with which the British and American planes flew their attacks.

The crews of the Allied aircraft could not be influenced, when instead of dropping their bombs on the factories, they did so on 'targets' away from them. They 'instinctively' evaded fire coming from the (destroyed, ploughed-up) works and, if possible, dropped their high-explosive bombs on undefended terrain.

—What do you mean by 'instinctive'? Do you mean a tensing of the stomach or a process in the brains of the aircrew?

—You've drawn my attention to an error. No individual in such an aircraft, a kind of flying industrial plant, a factory in other words, can change the flight course 'instinctively'. If the pilot, because of a tensing of the stomach muscles communicated to his hands, manages to alter course, then that is corrected by the co-pilot. We have the suspicion that the whole 'grotesque machine', the individual bomber and the totality of the squadron are centrally controlled. Consequently each evasive action directed by human muscles or impulses was paralysed and to that extent the instinctive action of an individual was out of the question. 'Instinctive' here means 'a feeling that takes hold of the whole crew'.

—And something like that cannot be influenced by 'leadership'?

—Not by planned leadership.

—And that led to massive quantities of bombs being dropped on the town instead of on the factories next to the town?

—They were already ploughed over.

We witnesses on the other shore, that is, in Switzerland, had an amateur film camera, an automatic, loaded with a film roll from 1938. We filmed what happened. It was as if we were obsessed by the sight of the machines disappearing in the lake. With the help of the camera we wanted to capture 'the moment', be able to repeat it. There was no one in Switzerland, however, who could have developed the film. According to the camera instructions of 1938 the film cassette had to be removed and sent to Dessau. A guarantee declaring that the copy would be returned by post was also enclosed. The costs of the return postage were included in the price of the cassette. The factory in Dessau, which promised this service, had long since been destroyed. Hence the film remained in the camera and could not be developed after the war either, as the technology of 1938 was never reproduced in such a way that it would have been able to copy the old 'material'. Only what we had seen with our own eyes showed us the disappearance of the giant aircraft after they had come down from a great height. This impression never faded from our long-term memory. The unsteady flight and the beginning of the fall to the lake surface had taken one and a half minutes. The crash itself and the submersion in the water: no more than 30 seconds.

The Gleam in the Enemy's Eye

During the war the Ufa[6] cameramen attached increasing importance to perfecting 'eye light'. A spotlight shining from the same direction as the camera throws light into the actor's eyes, producing a reflection that makes the eye bright.

---

6 Universum Film AG. The largest German film company before 1933, it was effectively nationalized during the war and had monopoly on filmmaking in the Third Reich. [Trans.]

This effect is shot in close-up for close-combat scenes and battles between mounted knights (but also for the first meeting of lovers) and using a fixed camera. For action scenes of battles such a close-up is inserted for seconds at a time. Then there's a gleam in the enemy's eye. No montage is necessary to emphasize the impression of a gleam in the eye of the lover.

In the practice of modern war hardly anyone saw a gleam in the enemy's eye. One rarely saw the enemy at close quarters— and in the air war virtually never. Eyes might perhaps make an impression at executions. After 1941 the air war as a subject of feature films was pushed into the background in Ufa's plans. Scripts were repeatedly proposed whose starting point was the experience of the bombed and of the crews manning the anti-aircraft guns. With a positive message. By the end of the war none of them had been realized. The censors assumed that showing such experiences would make the national comrades unfit for the demands of wartime. Scenes by candlelight in air-raid shelters would in themselves have been very suited to perfecting the technique of 'eye light'.

Total Toothache /
From the Beginnings of the Arms Race in the Air between the Two World Wars (1923)

The test subjects from Libya and Calabria, their upkeep cheap, as the Italian General Douhet put it in his paper at the Kaiserhof Hotel in Berlin, reliably displayed the predicted violent symptoms of pain as soon as the dust came into contact with the mucous membranes of their mouths. It was also sufficient if the mucous membranes of the nose were irritated by a few particles of the material. Nevertheless, continued the general, one should not consider the development of this weapon as concluded. It would certainly be a weapon that decided the outcome of a war. It would help decide future air wars. Experiments in the test area, however, had already shown that with the materials so far discovered it would be almost impossible to spray a whole town with the chemical in such a way that a sufficient number of mouths would be reached simultaneously causing a panic-like terror (that is, the moment deciding the battle) to ensue. Before that happened these people would find makeshift means to help themselves and, for example, hold dampened cloths in front of mouth and nose. The test subjects had to be instructed to keep their mouths open, since otherwise the 'rain of dust' would not have been very effective.

Under war conditions that was not an adequate method of proceeding.

The chemical 'weapon' consisted of a dry, very fine dust. Air resistance and wind scattered the armament in all directions, as soon as the substance was discharged from the aircraft. This was another problem, added the general. It was impossible to shovel the stuff out of the airplane in the face of the slipstream round it—the dust had to be 'sprayed'. In the experiments in the test area only small quantities reached a specific location on the ground in reasonable time.

Should the spraying or squirting begin when the plane was already three or four miles from the target? Should the target be calculated from the centre or the edge of a town? Does flying at low altitude place the crew at risk, because in such a position they themselves are reached by the harmful substance? Question upon question. The general repeated that the test stage had not been concluded with respect to any of these issues. A bonus, however, of this still-unfinished weapon was that the pain, once initiated, intensified of its own accord over the whole dental area. The brains of humans (thanks to their sociable and garrulous nature), said the general, are invariably capable of anticipation. If it is interrupted for a moment, the wave-like structure of pain is imagined all the more powerfully by the chorus of now inactive nerves.

It made no difference at all if one drew the teeth of the test subjects. In that case the substance caused phantom pain.

For the time being, conceded the general, the planning was not part of air-war manoeuvres (as they were at present permitted on Italian state territory but not in the German Reich). In these manoeuvres one had got no further than the simpler conception of a bell jar of gas, spanning the enemy towns and cities. The heavy gas bubble lays itself reliably (in the comfortable posture of a St Bernard dog) over the terrain to be gassed and kills everything there, taking effect from bottom up and to the sides. Four war planes flying over the town from the four points of the compass and equipped with the appropriate containers from which the gas is poured would be sufficient, confirmed General Douhet, to feed the 'jar' for more than a day. Despite immediate success the 'blanketing' of a city should be maintained for several days, since, if the enemy knew about the weapon, then enclosed, gastight artefacts and gas masks could perhaps make survival possible for a certain period of time.

At five in the afternoon the meeting rooms in the Kaiserhof Hotel were all hired out. In 1923 the disposition of the bookings still displayed tolerance. A 'red' organization had hired one of the rooms. Next door: 'middle class' functions. All neighbours of the conference venue of the secret organization of which the participants in the air-war discussion were members. Seven-storey trolleys with toasted sandwiches were pushed along the corridors to the tearooms and also taken into the conference rooms.

In the war to come, asserted General Douhet, enemies would never come face-to-face on a battlefield. They would meet for the first time on neutral territory on the occasion of the unconditional capitulation of the side that had been chemically bombarded. Douhet's paper was a high point in the planning of long-range combat. Such long-range combat, said the general, is particularly suited to absolutely avoiding the horrors of the First World War.

News of Star Wars

Fire will rain down from the stars. The exact consistency of this rain was described in somewhat contradictory terms on the website of the prophet Fred Myerson of Minnesota. It was said that the fire would fall with the force of the facades of whole buildings, also in pieces the size of whole districts of towns. 'And that not from God's hand!'

The prophet found it difficult to express himself as he was writing his communications. His cup of coffee remained untouched. It was hard for him to say in what way Star Wars weapons would affect part of a city. Nor would caves and deserts and the open sea offer safety (i.e. to individuals and small groups). But whether the effect should be defined as a 'glowing arrow', as with a laser weapon, or more like a board or flake (as the substances came down), could not be concluded from the prophet's statement. His web page had many hits.

The prophet, however, was no religious fanatic, but the pseudonym of a high-ranking US general-staff officer, responsible for the Space-Based Weapons System in Tampa, Florida. He had strict orders not to divulge any of his knowledge. It is ultimately impossible, nevertheless, to uncouple a leading expert from the urge to publicly express his opinion. Hence this participant in the arms race was active on the web under a false name.

Between History and Natural History.
On the Literary Description of Total Destruction.
Remarks on Kluge*

W. G. SEBALD

. . . A comparison of Hermann Kasack's novel *The City Beyond the River*[1] with Hans Erich Nossack's prose text 'The End: Hamburg 1943'[2] shows that, if it is to be valid, the attempt to write a literary description of collective catastrophes necessarily breaks with the fictional form of the novel indebted to a bourgeois world view. At the time when these works were written, the implications for the technique of writing could not yet be foreseen. They become increasingly clear, however, as literature in West Germany addresses the debacle of recent German history. Alexander Kluge's extremely complex and at first sight heterogeneous book *Neue Geschichten. Hefte 1–18, Unheimlichkeit der Zeit*,[3]

* From 'Zwischen Geschichte und Naturgeschichte. Versuch über die literarische Beschreibung totaler Zerstörung mit Anmerkungen zu Kasack, Nossack und Kluge'. First published in *Orbis litterarum* 37(4) (1982): 345–66. Here, only pp. 359–66 are translated as republished in W. G. Sebald, *Campo Santo* (Sven Meyer ed.) (Munich, 2003), pp. 69–100. A slightly shorter extract was translated by Anthea Bell in W. G. Sebald, *Campo Santo* (London, 2005) pp. 89–100. A greatly abbreviated version, also translated by Anthea Bell, is to be found in W. G. Sebald, *On the Natural History of Destruction* (London, 2003) [German title *Luftkrieg und Literatur* (Munich 1999)]. The extract translated here takes account of the lengthy quotations from *The Air Raid on Halberstadt on 8 April 1945* and of the changes to the text as noted in 'Sources'. [Trans.]

1 'Die Stadt hinter dem Strom' (1947); English translation 1953. [Trans.]

2 'Der Untergang (1948); English translation 2006. [Trans.]

3 *New Stories. Numbers 1–18*, '*Uncanniness of Time*'. A slightly different version of the book is contained in Alexander Kluge, *Chronik der Gefühle*, VOL. 2 (Frankfurt/Main, 2000), pp. 9–453. [Trans.]

published in 1977, consequently refuses the temptation of integration perpetuated by the familiar forms of literature. Rather, it presents the preparatory collection and organization of the historical and fictional text and picture material in the author's notebooks without further deferral and does so less with the claim of producing an opus than as an example of literary work in progress. If this procedure undermines the traditional idea of a creative subject, ordering the discrepancies in the wide field of reality in a representation, then that does not mean that subjective concern and subjective engagement, the starting point of imaginative effort, have been invalidated. Instead, the second number of *New Stories*, which deals with the air raid on Halberstadt on 8 April 1945, has the character of a model study. The reader may learn from it how personal involvement in the collectively experienced course of events, also still of crucial importance to Nossack, can only be meaningfully condensed, at least heuristically, through analytical historical investigations, through reference to the prehistory of the events as well as to later developments up to the present day and to possible future perspectives. Kluge, who grew up in Halberstadt, was 13 at the time of the raid. 'The form of the impact of a high explosive bomb is never forgotten,' he writes in the foreword to the stories, and 'I was there, when on 8 April 1945 something like that exploded 30 feet away.'[4] Nowhere else in the text does the author refer directly to himself. His relationship to the destruction of his home town is that of a research into lost time by means of which the traumatic and shocking experiences which, by complicated processes of repression, were consigned to amnesia, are brought over into a present-day reality in fact conditioned by the buried

4 *Neue Geschichten. Hefte 1–18, 'Unheimlichkeit der Zeit'* (Frankfurt/Main, 1977), p. 9.

history. In direct contrast to Nossack, the retrospective investigation of what took place is not determined by what the author has seen with his own eyes and by what he can still remember, but by the course of events related to his life then and now. As remains to be shown, the intention of the text as a whole is based on the insight that experience in the real sense was simply not possible because of the overwhelming rapidity and totality of the destruction and can only occur by way of the detour of later learning.

The literary documentation of the air raid on Halberstadt also possesses an exemplary character from another point of view. This is particularly the case whenever the question as to the 'sense' of the methodical destruction of whole towns and cities is raised. Authors like Kasack and Nossack leave it aside, partly because of lack of information or because of a feeling of personal guilt. But also because they mystified the destruction as God-given judgement and as long-overdue punishment. It is presumably indisputable today that the strategy pursued by the Allied air forces, of the area bombing of as many German towns and cities as possible, was unjustifiable in terms of military purpose. In that case—as Kluge's text shows—the destruction, the horrifying devastation, of a middling town, quite insignificant strategically or as a centre of arms production, must make the dynamic of the factors determining technological warfare appear questionable in the highest degree. Kluge's report includes an interview by a correspondent of the [Swiss] *Neue Zürcher Zeitung* with a senior staff officer. Both are flying on the raid as observers. Primarily at issue in Kluge's extract is the question of 'morale bombing', the intention of which is clarified by Brigadier General Williams [in the text as translated: Brigadier William B. Roberts] with reference to the official doctrine on which the air raids are based. To the question 'Do you bomb for moral reasons or do you bomb morale?' the officer replies: 'We bomb morale. The spirit of resistance must be removed from the given population by the destruction of the town.' Later he concedes, however, that this morale cannot be hit by bombs.

> Morale is evidently not situated in the heads or here (*points to the solar plexus*), but is to be found somewhere between the persons or populations of the various towns. That's been researched and is well known at staff headquarters [. . .] There is evidently nothing at all in heart or head. That's anyway plausible. Because those people who are smashed to pieces don't think or feel anything. And those, who despite all the measures taken, escape the attack evidently don't bear the impressions of the disaster with them. They take all kinds of baggage with them, but it seems they leave the impressions of the moment of the attack behind.[5]

5 See pp. 58–9 of this volume. The conclusions the reader can draw from these 'statements' agree with the arguments Solly Zuckerman published in his autobiographical report 'From Apes to Warlords' (London, 1978). During the war, Lord Zuckerman was scientific advisor to the British government on questions of air-war strategy. He personally made considerable efforts to persuade Bomber Command under Air Marshal 'Bomber' Harris not to persist with the strategy of blanket destruction. Instead, he advocated selective attacks aimed at the enemy's communications system which he was convinced would have brought the war to an end earlier and with far fewer victims. This incidentally coincides with the considerations on the subject presented in Speer's memoirs. [Hitler appointed Albert Speer Reich Minister for Armaments and War Production in February 1942.— Trans.] Lord Zuckerman writes: 'As we now know, bombing at about a hundred times the intensity of anything ever suffered by European cities during the Second World War at no moment broke the spirit of the people of Vietnam against whom the American forces were fighting between 1964 and 1973. In those nine years, 7 million tons of bombs were dropped on South Vietnam (which received about half the total), North Vietnam, Laos and Cambodia—three times the total tonnage of British, American and German bombs dropped on European soil in the Second

Nossack gives us no kind of information about the motives and causes prior to the act of destruction. Kluge, on the other hand, attempts, both in this case, as in his earlier Stalingrad book,[6] to make the organizational build-up of such a catastrophe comprehensible and shows how, for reasons of administrative inertia, it continues to take its course even in the face of greater knowledge. Hence it becomes impossible to pose the question of ethical responsibility.

Kluge's text begins with a description of the complete inadequacy of all socially predetermined ways of behaving in the face of the irrevocably unfolding catastrophe. Frau Schrader, the experienced manageress of the Capitol Cinema, sees the sequence of her Sunday programme, tried and tested over the years—on that 8 April a film directed by Gustav Ucicky, starring Paula Wessely, Peter Petersen and Attila Hörbiger is scheduled—wrecked by the overriding organization of the destruction. She makes panicky attempts to create order somehow, perhaps clear away the rubble in time for the 2 p.m. showing. This vividly illustrates, by way of the extreme discrepancy between the active and passive fields of action of the catastrophe, the almost humorous insight, for both reporter and reader, that 'the devastation of the right-hand side of the cinema stood in no meaningful or dramatic relationship to the film.'[7] The emergency

World War' ('Warlords', p. 148), which varies his argument as to the objective pointlessness of *area bombing*. He also remarks that after the war, after he had inspected the effects of the air raids on German cities, he intended writing a report under the title 'The Natural History of Destruction' for the journal *Horizon*, edited by Cyril Connolly. The plan, unfortunately, was never carried out.

6 See Alexander Kluge, 'Schlachtbeschreibung'. First published 1964, revised edition 1978, both Frankfurt/Main; also in Alexander Kluge, *Chronik der Gefühle*, VOL. 1, pp. 509–793.

7 See p. 1.

deployment of a company of soldiers appears similarly irrational. They are ordered to dig up and sort 'about 100 in-part
terribly mutilated bodies, some out of the earth, some out of
identifiable pits that had made up the shelter,'[8] without having
any idea what purpose this operation could still serve under the
prevailing circumstances. The unknown photographer who is
challenged by an army patrol and maintains 'that he had wanted
to record the burning town, his hometown, at this moment of
its misfortune',[9] adheres, just like Frau Schrader, to what his professional instinct suggests to him. His intention of documenting
the end is only not absurd because his pictures—Kluge has
included them in the text as photos 1–6—have come down to
us and that, given his possible prospects at the time, was hardly
to be expected. The tower observers, Frau Arnold and Frau
Zacke, are provided with folding chairs, torches, thermos bottles,
beer, packets of sandwiches, binoculars and two-way radios.
Even as the tower beneath them appears to move they continue
whispering their information, reciting it as if they were giving
answers at school, and don't tear themselves away from their
assignment until the wooden frame inside the tower has begun
to burn. Frau Arnold ends her life under a pile of rubble of
stones and burnt wood on which rests a bell, while Frau Zacke
waits for hours with a broken thigh before she is rescued by sur-
vivors from bombed-out houses on Martiniplan. A wedding
party at the Horse Inn is already buried 12 minutes final warning, along with its social differences—the bridegroom 'from a
property-owning family in Cologne', the bride 'from the Lower
Town' in Halberstadt.[10] These and numerous other examples

8 See p. 5.
9 See p. 6.
10 See p. 18.

making up the text show how, even when faced with the catastrophe, the individuals and groups affected are incapable of
judging the scale of the threat and of deviating from socially prescribed behaviour. Since in the catastrophe, as Kluge empha-
sizes, clock time and 'the sensory processing of time are
diverging', only 'with the brains of tomorrow' would it be possible to 'think up practical emergency measures in these quarters
of an hour'.[11] This divergence, which can never be balanced,
even by 'the brains of tomorrow' confirms Brecht's remark that
human beings learn as much from catastrophes as laboratory
rabbits about biology.[12] From which it follows that the degree of
human autonomy in the face of the actual or potential destruction contrived by humankind is, in terms of the history of the
species, no greater than that of the rodent in the scientist's cage.
This is a constellation that, in turn, makes it comprehensible why
the speaking and thinking machines, about which Stanislaw Lem
writes, ask themselves whether humans can really think at all or
whether they merely simulate this activity from which they derive
their self-image.[13]

It may be that the human capacity for processing experience, determined socially and by natural history, excludes the
possibility that the species could escape a catastrophe it has itself
caused, unless quite by chance. That does not at all mean, however, that a retrospective examination of the conditions of

11 See p. 23.

12 See the text 'Wuppertal 1945' by Robert Wolfgang Schnell in *Vaterland, Mut-
tersprache: Deutsche Schriftsteller und ihr Staat seit 1945* (K. Wagenbach, W.
Stephan and M. Krüger eds) (Berlin, 1979) p. 29, which quotes this remark by
Brecht in a context relevant here.

13 See Stanislaw Lem, 'Imaginäre Grösse' (Frankfurt/Main, 1981) p. 74. English
translation: *Imaginary Magnitude* (San Diego, 1984).

destruction would be futile. Rather, the learning process that takes place subsequently—and that is the *raison d'être* of Kluge's text compiled 30 years after the event—presents the only possibility of directing the hopes and wishes arising in human beings towards the anticipation of a future that is not already occupied by fear resulting from repressed experience. Gerda Baethe, an elementary-school teacher, has something of the kind in mind. Admittedly, as the author notes, to realize a 'strategy from below' such as the one Gerda imagines, 'Since 1918, 70,000 determined teachers, all like her, would have had to teach hard for 20 years in each of the countries involved in the First World War.'[14] The perspective that opens up here for a possibly different course of history can be understood, despite the ironic tone, as a serious appeal for a future elaborated in defiance of all calculations of probability. It is precisely Kluge's description of the social organization of the disaster, programmed by the constantly intensified errors of history forever dragged along in its wake, that contains the implicit hope that a proper understanding of the catastrophes we arrange would be the primary condition of the social organization of happiness. On the other hand, it can hardly be denied that the planned build-up of the misfortune, which Kluge derives historically from the development of the industrial relations of production, makes it more or less impossible any longer to justify the abstract principle of hope. The development of the strategy of the air war in its prodigious complexity, the professionalization of the bomber crews as 'trained war experts', the necessity, wherever possible, of excluding in these professionals occasional personal perceptions, 'e.g. the tidiness of the fields below; rows of houses, blocks of buildings; orderly quarters reminiscent of home',[15]

14 See p. 32.
15 See p. 36.

managing the psychological problems as to how the interest of the crews in their task, despite the completely abstract nature of their function, is to be maintained, the question of how the planned sequence of an operational cycle in which '200 middling-sized industrial plants'[16] fly towards a town can be guaranteed, technically ensuring that the dropping of the bombs produces extensive fires and fire storms—all these aspects, viewed by Kluge from the point of view of the organizers, reveal that the planning of such destruction involves such quantities of ingenuity, labour power and capital that, given the pressure of the accumulated potential, the plan must be realized. The central point of Kluge's exposition in this respect is to be found in an interview dated 1952, and interpolated in the text, between Kunzert, a reporter from Halberstadt, who had made his way to the West with the British troops in 1945, and Brigadier Frederick L. Anderson [in the text as translated: Brigadier Wesley C. Anderson]. The latter tries, with some patience, to answer, from the perspective of the military professional, the naive question about whether the timely raising of a large white flag, sewn from six sheets, on the tower of St Martin's Church, could have averted the attack on the town. Anderson's explanations, at first confined to the sphere of military logistics, as to why such an action would have been quite pointless, culminate finally in a statement in which the notoriously irrational peak of all rationalist argumentation becomes evident. He points out that the bombs carried are 'expensive stuff'. 'And you can't drop it on the hills or the open country, after it's been produced with so much labour power at home.'[17] The consequence of the overriding production pressures (summed up here), which—with the best will in the world!—neither responsible

---

16 See third footnote in the box on p. 43.
17 See p. 55.

individuals or even groups are able to evade, is the ruined town as it is spread out in the photo on p. 80 in this volume. The picture bears as caption the following quote from Marx: '*We see how the history of* industry *and its* objective *existence, are the* open *book of* man's essential powers, *human* psychology *made present and perceptible* . . .'[18]

The reconstruction of the catastrophe that Kluge achieves in this way, and in much greater detail than could be recapitulated here, may be equated with the disclosure of the rationalist structure of something millions of people experienced as an irrational blow of fate. It is almost as if Kluge were taking up the challenge that the allegorical figure in Nossack's *Interview mit dem Tode* issues to his interlocutor: 'If you like, you can take a look at my factory. There's nothing secret about it. It's the lack of secrecy that's the point. Do you understand?'[19] Death, presented in this text as a persuasive businessman, explains with the same ironic patience which characterizes the attitude of Brigadier Anderson that, basically, everything is just a question of organization, an organization that is not only manifested in collective catastrophes but also in all spheres of everyday life. If one wanted to get behind the secret, then nothing more is necessary than a visit to a tax office or a ration-card distribution office. It is these links between the incredible scale of destruction 'produced' by humans and daily experienced reality that are the pivotal point of Kluge's didactic intentions. Kluge continuously reminds the reader, even in the nuances of his complicated speech compositions, that only the maintenance of a critical dialectic between

18 See p. 80; emphasis added.
19 Hans Erich Nossack, *Interview mit dem Tode* (Frankfurt/Main, 1972), p. 121.
20 See Andrew Bowie, *Problems of Historical Understanding in the Modern Novel.* Thesis typescript (Norwich, 1979) and an outstanding work whose concluding chapter discusses Kluge.

present and past can set a learning process in motion which is not from the start doomed to have a 'fatal outcome'. As Andrew Bowie has emphasized,[20] the texts with which Kluge seeks to promote this aim correspond neither to the pattern of retrospective historiography nor to the narrative of the novel. Nor do they try to provide a philosophy of history. Rather, they are a form of reflection on all these modalities of our understanding of the world. Kluge's art, if one wishes to apply the term, consists in making discernible *the details* of the broad outline of the fatal tendency of history until now. This is evident in the reference to the toppled trees in the Halberstadt town park, 'which in the eighteenth century, when they were planted, [. . .] had been the home of silk worms'.[21] Likewise in the following passage:

> **[9 Domgang]** In the windows, just after the air raid, there was, knocked over, a range of tin soldiers. The remainder, 12,400 men in all, Ney's III. Corps, desperately advancing through the Russian winter towards the easternmost stragglers of the Grande Armée, was packed away in boxes in cupboards. It was set up once a year in Advent. Only Herr Gramert himself could place the mass of soldiers in the correct order. In panic-stricken flight away from this apple of his eye he has been struck on the head by a burning beam in Krebsschere Lane, is unable to make any further decisions. The apartment at 9 Domgang, with all the marks of Gramert's personal style, lies quiet and intact for another two hours, except that it grows ever hotter in the course of the afternoon. At about 5 p.m., like the tin figures in their boxes, which melt into lumps, it has burnt out.[22]

21 See p. 5.
22 See p. 24.

It would hardly be possible to write a more succinct parable [Lehrstück] than this. In Kluge's form of presentation, the vectors with which he provides his documentary material allows the quoted matter to be translated into our present. Kluge 'does not allow the data to stand merely as an account of a past catastrophe,' writes Bowie, 'the most unmediated document [. . .] loses its unmediated character via the processes of reflection the text sets up. History is no longer the past but also the present in which the reader must act.'[23] The instruction pursued by Kluge's mode of writing about the past and present conditions of the reader's existence as about the possible prospects in our future prove him to be an author working at the outer edge of a civilization, one to all appearances heading for self-destruction, on the regeneration of the collective memory of his contemporaries, who 'despite an inborn pleasure in telling stories had, precisely within the contours of the destroyed areas of the town, lost the psychic strength to remember.'[24] It is probably only the preoccupation with this didactic task that enables Kluge not to give in any further to the temptation of a purely natural historical interpretation of recent historical developments, as manifest in the recurring elements of prescient *science fiction* superimposed on his texts. It holds him back from interpreting history in the way that Lem, for example, does, as the long-evident catastrophic consequence of an anthro-pogenesis, based from the very start on evolutionary mistakes, and marked by man's over-complicated physiology, by the development of his hypertrophic mind and of his technical means of production.

23 Bowie, *Problems of Historical Understanding*, p. 295.
24 See p. 83.

SOURCES

'Der Luftangriff auf Halberstadt am 8. April 1945'
(The Air Raid on Halberstadt on 8 April 1945)

First published in Alexander Kluge, *Neue Geschichten. Hefte 1-18. 'Unheimlichkeit der Zeit'* (Frankfurt/Main, 1977) pp. 33–106. Reprinted in slightly altered form in Alexander Kluge, *Chronik der Gefühle*, VOL. 2 (Frankfurt/Main, 2000), pp. 27–82.

The present translation is taken from the one-volume edition, Alexander Kluge, *Der Luftangriff auf Halberstadt am 8. April 1945* (Frankfurt/Main, 2008).

All changes in the English translation with respect to these last two editions were made either by the author or with his permission. [Trans.]

'Was heisst "wirklich" im nachhinein? 17 weitere Geschichten zum Luftkrieg'
(What Does 'Really' Mean in Retrospect? 17 More Stories of the Air War)

'Libellen des Todes' (Dragonflies of Death)
From Alexander Kluge, *Tür an Tür mit einem anderen Leben* (Frankfurt/Main, 2006) pp. 92–3.

'Kommentar zu Libellen des Todes' (Commentary on Dragonflies of Death)
From *Tür an Tür*, p. 94.

'Die Libelle' (The Dragonfly)
From Alexander Kluge, *Die Lücke, die der Teufel lässt* (Frankfurt/Main, 2003), p. 100.

'Die langen Wege der Einsicht' (The Long Paths to Knowledge)
From *Tür an Tür*, p. 590.

'Was heisst "wirklich" im nachhinein?' (What Does 'Really' Mean in Retrospect?)
From *Tür an Tür*, pp. 242–3.

'Liebe 1944' (Love 1944)
From *Tür an Tür*, p. 491. English translation also available in Alexander Kluge/Gerhard Richter, *December* (London, 2012), pp. 51–2.

'Kooperatives Verhalten' (Cooperative Behaviour)
From *Chronik der Gefühle*, VOL. 2, pp. 929–30.

'Brände im Inneren von Menschen' (Fires inside People)
From *Die Lücke, die der Teufel lässt*, pp. 785–6, titled 'Soviel Mord war nie'.

'Zootiere im Bombenkrieg' (Zoo Animals in the Air Raids)
From *Die Lücke, die der Teufel lässt*, p. 778. English translation also available in Alexander Kluge, *The Devil's Blind Spot* (New York, 2004) pp. 34–5.

'Was hält freiwillige Taten zusammen?' (What Holds Voluntary Actions Together?)
From *Chronik der Gefühle*, VOL. 1, pp. 921–7.

'Feuerlöscherkommandant W. Schönecke berichtet' (Fire-Brigade Commander W. Schönecke Reports)
From *Chronik der Gefühle*, VOL. 1, pp. 451–3.

'Vorfeld der Katastrophe' (The Run-Up to the Catastrophe)
From *Die Lücke, die der Teufel lässt*, pp. 316–17.

'Wie die "fliegenden Festungen" im Bodensee verschwanden' (How the 'Flying Fortresses' Disappeared in Lake Constance)
From Alexander Kluge, *Geschichten vom Kino* (Frankfurt/Main, 2007), pp. 229–31.

'Das Blitzen im Auge des Gegners' (The Gleam in the Enemy's Eye)
From *Der Luftangriff auf Halberstadt am 8. April 1945* (2008), p. 124.

'Der totale Zahnschmerz' (Total Toothache)
From *Der Luftangriff auf Halberstadt am 8. April 1945* (2008), pp. 125–7.

'Nachricht vom Sternenkrieg' (News of Star Wars)
From *Der Luftangriff auf Halberstadt am 8. April 1945* (2008), pp. 127–8.